When the Marquess Returns

A Legend To Love

Alanna Lucas

Dianne,

Enjoy the
Twins!

[signature]

ISBN 978-0-9985314-3-4

Sebastiani Press
PO Box 1234
Simi Valley, Ca 93062

Cover by Teresa Spreckelmeyer, The Midnight Muse

For Anna and Emilio
Grazie per il tuo amore e supporto

Author's Note

I've always had a fascination with Rome—it is one of my favorite cities. When deciding on which legend I would choose for *A Legend To Love Series*, I instantly thought of the tale of Romulus and Remus. There are several slight variations of the legend, but for the purpose of *When the Marquess Returns*, I followed the most well-known, adding my own twists, and, of course, a Happily Ever After.

The Legend:

In Roman mythology Romulus and Remus, the founders of Rome, were the sons of Rhea Silvia and Mars. According to legend, their story begins even before their conception when Rhea Silvia—the daughter of King Numitor, was forced to become a Vestal Virgin after her uncle, Amulius, overthrew the king.

However, Rhea Silvia soon became pregnant and gave birth to twin sons. Seeing this as a threat, Amulius ordered the infants to be drowned in the Tiber River. But the servant charged with the gruesome task took pity on the infants, placed them into a basket onto the Tiber, where they were carried to safety. They were found by a she-wolf, who suckled them until they were discovered by a shepherd and his wife, Acca Larentia, who raised the boys.

After learning their true identity, Romulus and Remus attacked King Amulius, and restored their grandfather to the throne. On April 21, 753 B.C., the twins decided to found a city on the site where they had been saved as infants. However, they became engaged in a petty quarrel after which it is believed that Romulus killed Remus. The city of Rome was named after Romulus.

Chapter One

London, May 1819

THE MOMENT MAXIMUS, his brother, and their adoptive mother entered the spacious hall of the grand theatre, curious eyes settled on them and murmurs encircled their small party.

Stares were commonplace whenever they entered a room, especially in this new environment. It had always been the case, although the novelty usually wore off within a couple of minutes. However, there was one lady in particular who kept her gaze centered on them, puzzlement streaked across her face. She tilted her brow, looking at them with uncertainty, almost as if she were trying to understand something. She didn't attempt to approach but continued to peer intently at them.

"Why is that woman staring at us?" Maximus questioned under his breath, barely able to keep the annoyance at bay.

"Perhaps she's never seen twins before," Lucius rebuffed.

Maximus and Lucius were not just twins, they were identical and—according to the local girls in the small village close to their childhood home near Plymouth— were "two of the most handsome men alive, and completely swoon-worthy". It was a moniker that Maximus did not care for, never had and probably never would. He'd rather be known for his intelligence, or skill with a horse, or knowledge of multiple languages, not for something as fleeting as appearance.

"Perhaps you remind her of someone. Just ignore," Larentia, their mother, said with nonchalance and a slight wave of her hand. "These women of the *ton* are often far too absorbed in gossip. Besides, we've only just arrived in Town. It couldn't possibly have anything to do with us."

"Miss St. Albans!" a cheerful voice crescendoed above the crowd bringing even further attention to their party. A rather plump woman dressed in deep purple scurried towards them. "You've finally returned to London."

"Lady Kenton," Larentia took the woman's hands in her own. "It has been too long, my dearest friend."

"Twenty-three years too long to be exact." The woman's warm smile settled on Maximus and his brother. "These must be your adopted sons. It is a pleasure to meet you both at long last. Larentia has written to me often of your adventures. Tell me, how did you enjoy your time on the Continent?"

Their time touring Europe felt like a lifetime ago. When their adoptive grandfather announced he wanted Maximus and Lucius to follow in his footsteps and embark on the Grand Tour, the brothers were just nineteen and—in Maximus's opinion—naïve about the world beyond Plymouth. It had been a time of great personal growth for each of them. He'd enjoyed visiting new places, experiencing local customs, honing his drafting skills, and spending time with his brother, but he'd always longed for more. However, before he could conclude what 'more' encompassed, they'd been summoned home.

So much had happened since they'd returned two years ago.

"It was most enjoyable," Maximus answered in a tone he hoped did not invite further questions. He was not in the mood for reminiscing, for sharing those intimate details of their travels, with someone he'd just met.

His brother on the other hand...

"I particularly enjoyed the opera in Milan, *e le belle donne*," Lucius said before adding his infamously charming smile that quite frequently landed him in trouble.

"*Ricorda il nostro accordo*," Maximus warned under a hushed tone as Lady Kenton watched their exchange with interest. The brothers had already argued once today about Lucius's indiscretions since arriving in London a few days previous.

Lucius raised a brow in defiance, but kept his tone jovial. "*Lei non capisce l'italiano.*"

"Oh my, and you both speak Italian?" A slight giggle escaped Lady Kenton's mouth as a deep blush stained her entire face. Turning back to Larentia, she said, "I have not a clue what they are saying, however, I do believe the mamas had best keep a close watch on their daughters with your sons in Town this season."

Larentia shot Maximus and Lucius her best "behave yourself" warning before clearing her throat. "The play is about to begin."

"Oh yes, and it should be quite a spectacular performance this evening. Madame Hébert is performing the aria this evening." The trio followed Lady Kenton up the grand staircase toward her box, passing even more curious eyes. "We'll have plenty of time to get acquainted later."

The gentle hum of conversation and general merriment that had filled the theatre lessened—only slightly—as the production began. Even as Maximus tried to focus on the stage and ignore the chatter echoing across the vast gold and green space, his mind wandered, contemplating the disagreement he'd had with his brother earlier regarding Lucius's current paramour. The woman in question had actually snuck into their townhome and cornered Maximus, believing *he* was Lucius. Then, upon discovering they were identical twins, offered her services to both brothers.

Maximus lost his temper with the woman, which angered his brother.

Why did he and his twin have to constantly be at odds? It never had been this way until their grandfather had passed away and they'd learned they would have to leave St. Albans Manor for London. Looking back, something had begun to change with Lucius that day.

Maximus adjusted himself for the umpteenth time, swiveling this way and that, trying to find a comfortable position. It wasn't that the seat was uncomfortable, or that he could even place blame on his surroundings— despite all the stares, it was that *he* was uncomfortable; uncomfortable and restless.

He stretched his legs and, in the process, made contact with his brother's chair. Two glaring blue eyes met his. "What is wrong with you?" Lucius's scold rumbled above the performance.

He shook his head, brushing off his brother's question. They'd already had one argument this evening, and he would be damned if they had another— and this one not in the privacy of their home. He couldn't do that to Larentia...again.

Damn. Why couldn't he relax?

He turned his focus to the stage, trying to enjoy... Hell, he couldn't even recall what he was supposed to be enjoying. A long sigh escaped his lips, earning a glare from all in their box. He attempted to adjust his legs again, this time kicking his brother's ankle. Lucius eyed him with annoyance, his mouth opened as if to argue, then he snapped it shut.

This was pointless.

Maximus left the box before he annoyed his brother further, and ducked into the hall, his muscles instantly relaxing. Perhaps he just wasn't used to the city. Except for those couple of years spent traveling across the Continent, he had spent little time in any city, much preferring quiet country life. A quick walk should ease whatever was plaguing him.

Strolling casually, ignoring the couple of theatregoers loitering at the far end of the hall, he began to make his way toward the grand staircase. Before he reached his destination, a muffled argument from one of the boxes halted his retreat.

No sooner had the sounds reached his ear when a woman stormed out of the box in question, colliding with him. He wrapped his arm about her waist to keep her from landing on the floor. They stood chest to chest, hearts beating rapidly.

"Oh," she gasped. "I..." Her words halted as she glanced up at him. Warm vanilla and sweet lavender encircled them.

Maximus stared into the most enticing eyes he'd ever seen—one emerald green, one deep brown. Her compelling eyes riveted him in place as his heart pounded against his chest anew.

Time halted, and energy surged between them. She stared at him with a tender longing.

Who was this woman?

Countless moments later, the lady spoke. "I apologize for ruining—"

"You didn't ruin anything," he quickly reassured her, but couldn't the find words to say more.

Her mouth curved into a beautiful smile, revealing matching dimples, which sent a whirlwind through his world. He'd always had a fondness for dimples. "I...I best be returning to my party."

"I suppose I should release you," he said with reluctance.

"Yes, I suppose," the words brushed past her pink lips with the same reluctance.

Several seconds passed before he actually did release her, his body instantly feeling the loss. Before he could ask her name, she retreated back into the box, leaving him wondering what the hell had just happened. If not for the remnants of lavender and vanilla clinging to his coat, he might have believed he dreamt the entire scene.

He paced a short length several times trying to convince himself he should *not* sneak into the box and discover her identity. *They had not been properly introduced. It would create a scene.* In the end, common sense won, and he decided it was best to rejoin his party.

Maximus took in a deep breath, the muscles tightening in chest, as he reluctantly walked back to his box.

"So nice of you to join us again." His brother's tone was laced with sarcasm as Maximus entered the loge. "I hope you've settled down."

His patience was being tested at every turn this evening. Before he could remark, Larentia stated, "Lady Kenton has offered to show us around Town later this week. Perhaps we may see the Egyptian Hall."

Maximus simply nodded as he took his seat. He had other things on his mind presently. He desperately wanted to discover more about the woman he'd encountered in the hall, and what had caused her to be so upset, and....

His heart sank. What if she was married and had quarreled with her husband? If that were the case, it was probably fortunate he hadn't barged in on her party. Before too long, he had conjured an entire scenario that had him enraged and wanting to call out the bastard who had upset her.

Damn. He needed to stay calm. He didn't even know her name. What if she wasn't married? How would he discover her identity without a proper introduction? He pondered the question for several minutes before an idea struck.

As soon as the play finished, he would rush to her box and casually bump into her again. It was a simple plan without the possibility of scandal. He would be able to talk to her again, and with any luck, acquire her name.

With his plan settled, he rather impatiently waited for the play to end. At least this time he knew what was disrupting his senses—a blonde-haired beauty, with the most intriguing eyes, four boxes away.

Loud clapping thundered through the theatre bringing him back to the present. Larentia and Lady Kenton were deep in conversation about the quality of the play and Madame Hébert's performance, while Lucius seemed distracted by something, or rather someone, near the stage.

Adrenaline rushed through his veins. There was no time to lose. He would worry about the next step once he found her again.

Emerging into the hall, excitement quickly gave way to frustration as his progress was hindered by several parties loitering in the hall engaging in lively talk about the evening's festivities, both on stage and in the audience. Maximus edged around them and waited near the box the lady had retreated to. With each passing minute, he became more anxious as more and more people filled the corridor. He watched as Larentia and Lady Kenton strolled past, and Lucius disappeared in the opposite direction. He could not be bothered with his brother's antics at the moment. Besides, he was his twin, not his keeper. He watched as the crowd dispersed and still no one emerged from box number four.

His insides turned as he struggled to formulate a new plan. Perhaps he could enter the loge, mistaking it for his own, claiming he'd forgotten...well, he didn't know what, he'd conjure some item when the time came. He maneuvered past the strolling guests, sucked in his breath, and pulled back the curtain.

Empty.

A heavy sigh escaped his lips. Where had she gone?

"Renovations on the cottage are almost complete. You'll finally be able to leave Warrington Hall."

"I enjoy spending time with Lady March," Sabina corrected her brother. Plus, she couldn't imagine being alone day after day, removed from Warrington Hall and those she held dear.

Titus ignored her comment, continuing on to extol the positives of the renovation. "I believe you will be most pleased with the small library," he said with much enthusiasm.

Since her lifelong dream to marry and have a family of her own would never be, it was nice to know that she would have a lovely cottage, far away from the gossips, to call her own. Despite her circumstances, she still fared better than most spinsters, thanks to her brother. He might be several years younger than her, but once he reached his majority, he had always ensured her future was secure.

Before she could express her appreciation for what Titus had arranged, her sister-in-law—Eunice, interfered. "The final steps into spinsterhood," she said with a snicker. "And a fitting end for the Cursed Heiress."

"Eunice, that's enough," Titus half-scolded. Sabina could not blame her brother for not taking a firmer approach with his wife. He had to endure her—and their mother—every day he took a breath, not to mention still being in need of an heir. She truly felt for him.

"You shouldn't take that tone with your wife," their mother said as she took Eunice's hand, lovingly folding it within her own.

Eunice raised a triumphant chin before taking another jab at Sabina's expense. "I suppose living the life of a spinster in the old hunting cottage *is* better than being at Lady March's side constantly." Eunice clearly had learned the disagreeable art of insulting Sabina from her husband's mother. For two women not related, the similarities and jibes were endless.

As if enduring her sister-in-law wasn't trying enough, Mother decided it was her turn to chime in, "I still can't quite comprehend how you managed to swindle His Grace and Lady March into letting you reside with them all these years."

Mustering what little bravado she had left in her soul, Sabina retorted, "Perhaps if you had been more—"

Mother's eyes turned ice cold and filled with hatred. "What? More of a mother?" She clutched her hand to her chest, her performance rivaling those of the actors on stage. "I was grieving the loss of my husband."

"And my father." Sabina shook her head, trying to erase the memory of that horrible day and her mother's unkind words. She did not want to suffer another lecture, followed by an argument, and conclude with more insults. Instead she settled for a plea. "I rarely see you and Titus. Do you not think it possible that we could have a pleasant evening just this once, Mother?"

"I agree with Sabina." For the second time that evening, her brother came to her defense, but she was certain he would pay the price later.

"Of course, you do," cried Eunice. "You always side with your *dearest* sister. You don't care for me." Sniffling, she buried her face in her hands.

Or sooner it would seem.

"There, there, Eunice, darling." Sabina's mother, the woman who'd given birth to her, who was supposed to love her, was comforting the instigator. Mother raised her gaze to Sabina. "Look what you've done." Hatred blazed in her eyes. "What have *I* done to deserve a daughter like you? I've been cursed since the day you were born."

The words seared straight through Sabina's heart, striking at her very core. Tears burned the corners of her eyes as she fought to control her breathing. One would think she would be used to the barbs after enduring so many years of them, but they still hurt. Since her father's passing, all she had ever wanted was her mother's love.

Desperate to escape, even if only for a moment to regain her composure, Sabina swallowed the hard lump in her throat, raised her chin, pulled back the curtain, rushed from their box none-too-gracefully, and straight into a wall. Only this wall was warm and smelled like a pleasant autumn afternoon in the country.

Firm arms wrapped about her waist, keeping her from falling. She glanced up into the most handsome face she'd ever seen.

"Oh...I...I'm..." She sounded like such a ninny instead of a woman of thirty.

She lost herself in the sea of his clear blue eyes. The theatre, her mother's cruel words, the constant stares, all faded away and settled into this one perfect moment. His warm hands penetrated through her satin dress, searing her skin and sent her heart thundering.

She tried to think of something intelligent—or at least somewhat witty—to say but she was not used to conversing with handsome men who disrupted her senses. "I...I apologize for ruining—"

"You didn't ruin anything," the handsome stranger's deep masculine voice quickly set her at ease. His fervent gaze stirred a long-forgotten flutter in her stomach.

She did not want the moment to end but did not want him to be caught with her either. She fought to control her swirling emotions. "I best be returning to my party."

"I suppose I should release you." It almost sounded like he didn't want to.

Her heart soared for a brief moment before reality pierced it with an arrow, sending it crashing to the ground. Although there was something familiar about him that she couldn't quite place, it was clear this gentleman was new to London, otherwise he would have already set her to her feet, bid adieu, and run the other way. The gossipmongers could be altogether too cruel to those who came near the Cursed Heiress.

"Yes, I suppose," she whispered. Despite the glorious feel of his warm hands holding her, it *was* for the best. Her life's path was clear, straight and narrow.

Although not quite ready to face her family, she slipped quietly into the box and took her seat, praying her mother might have some compassion for her frayed nerves.

"So, you've decided to return?" Mother's tone was hard and disapproving.

Sabina had hoped to have a pleasant visit with her brother, but current company made it impossible. Rigidly holding her tears in check, she tried to maintain her composure for peering eyes, tried to ignore her mother's slights and Eunice's harsh glare, tried to ignore the stares and hushed mockery from the gossipmongers, but she was only human.

Mustering whatever calmness still within her power, she politely excused herself. It was the one positive aspect to being a spinster—she could come and go as she pleased. No sooner had she retreated down the grand staircase than curious onlookers were weaving tales about the Cursed Heiress. She picked up her pace and never looked back.

Chapter Two

AFTER SPENDING A restless night begging the nightmare to stop, Sabina was exhausted, and her day was only just beginning. It was the same nightmare she'd had since she was seven years old, but this time...this time the nightmare was so much worse, threatening to swallow her whole. What could it mean? It had been years since her wild, tormented dreams had been *this* awful. An uneasiness settled in her stomach that had nothing to do with hunger.

What felt like hours later, she was as ready as she could possibly be to face the world. She didn't bother to take another glance at her appearance. She could barely focus on her steps, what with the pounding in her head. By the time she neared the breakfast room, not only was her head was aching badly, but her stomach was growling.

Smells of fresh-baked bread drifted into the hall, pulling her into the bright sunlit room. The promise of food eased some of the tension threatening to cause her world to spin onto its side. As was standard in the Duke of Warrington's house, the buffet overflowed with a variety of breads, cakes, coffee, tea, and warm chocolate. She made a plate and took her usual place near the head of the table. Warrington did not stand on formality when not entertaining.

Two nibbles of bread and not enough tea into her meal, Lady March strolled into the room. "Good morning, Sabina. Did you not enjoy visiting with your brother last evening?" Although her tone was pleasant, there was a layer of apprehension lacing her words.

Her mother's harsh words from the night before ricocheted off the banging in her head. Sabina rubbed her temple. *Don't think about her, she can't hurt you here.* Never one to complain about her family, she pasted on a smile and questioned, "Why do you believe the evening was poor?"

Sylvia strolled to the buffet, eyeing the assortment of delicacies. "You returned early and did not visit me."

Sabina had been so distraught because of the scene with her mother and sister-in-law that she'd retired the moment she'd got home. "I'm—"

"Dearest." Sabina raised her eyes at the endearment, meeting Sylvia's gaze. "You do not need to apologize. I'm just concerned."

It always warmed her heart how much Sylvia cared for her. They weren't related, or even close in age. Sorrow and grief had brought them together, friendship and love kept them together.

Icy fear twisted around her heart, as her mother's hurtful words played over in her mind. "Can I ask you something?"

Sylvia's brow creased with worry as she took the seat beside Sabina's. "Of course, dearest. You know you can talk to me about anything."

She took in a deep breath before the words poured form her mouth, "Do you ever regret taking me in all those years ago?"

"Why would you..." There was a brief pause as dawning settled in. "Oh, your mother." Sylvia's tone held only some of the disdain currently coursing through Sabina's veins. "No, my dearest. You've been a constant joy to both Warrington and I." She took Sabina's hand. "My only regret is that you never found love."

Thoughts of the gentleman she'd bumped into at the theatre, and the way he'd smiled at her, rushed to the forefront of Sabina's thoughts banishing the unpleasantness with her mother. Warmth filled her

cheeks and caressed her body. He was without a doubt
the most handsome man...

Lightning struck her thoughts. Ever since the
encounter, she'd been trying to place him. "There was a
man at the theatre who reminded me of someone, and
it just occurred to me whom. Is one of Warrington's
nephews in Town?"

"I don't believe so." Sylvia leaned forward with
great interest. "Perhaps it was one of Lachlan's sons.
They're not due to arrive until next week, but perhaps
they arrived early."

Sabina couldn't restrain the giggle. "If it was, the
mamas of the *ton* best lock up their daughters, bolt the
door and, post guards." She paused for a moment,
remembering the feel of the gentleman's hand on her
back as he kept her from falling, and the look in his
eyes as he held her in place. He might have looked like
one of the Duke's nephews, but he certainly did not act
like one. He hadn't taken advantage of the situation or
suggested anything untoward, and there was nothing
rakish about him. She shrugged off her first
assumption. "I suppose it was just someone who
reminded me of His Grace."

"Good morning, Lady March, Miss Teverton."
Picus, His Grace's most trusted servant— although
Sabina would not really call Picus a servant—greeted
them. Picus was more like a confidant-cum-valet-cum-
investigator. "Who reminds you of His Grace, and
please don't ruin the promise of a good day and inform
me that Lord Lachlan's sons have arrived early?"

Sabina and Sylvia giggled in unison. Poor Picus.
Quite frequently he had to repair any damages
Warrington's nephews caused.

Sabina did not know all Warrington's relatives, but
over the course of the past twenty plus years, she had
heard many fascinating stories involving the
Warrington men, and had even met quite a few of
them. They all seemed to bear the same remarkable

dark hair and blue eyes. "I encountered a gentleman last evening who had similar coloring to one of His Grace's relations."

"Could you tell me more about him?"

Ever since the Duke's grandsons were kidnapped more than twenty years previous, Picus and Lord Daniel—His Grace's younger son—had investigated every lead, no matter how small or impossible. It was the reason they returned to Town this season.

Warrington had received a cryptic message from the Duke of Rhuddlan informing him that twins, bearing a strong family resemblance, had recently departed Plymouth for London. Several days later, he received a similar letter from his friend, Lord Richard Somerset, who'd spotted the pair at a coaching inn near London. These were vague leads at best, but ones that still required investigation.

"He looked quite similar to His Grace, just a younger version and taller." Sabina had always thought the Duke a handsome gentleman, and despite the sadness that marred his features, he had aged gracefully. His once dark hair had greyed with the heartache he'd endured since first his grandsons were stolen in the dead of night, and then his eldest son was killed in a carriage accident.

"Was their anyone else with him? Did you speak with him? Did you happen to see his direction after the play ended?" Picus's questions turned almost desperate. The twenty-third anniversary of when Lord Zachary and Lord Richard were taken had come and gone, and still there was no clue as to what had happened, but the family had never given up hope.

Far too embarrassed about the episode with her mother and sister-in-law, Sabina skipped to the part where she bumped into the mysterious gentleman. She was used to the questioning and took no offense, trying to provide as much detail as she could. "I needed some air, slipped out part way through the first act, and encountered the gentleman in the hall. He was alone, so I am unsure who he attended the theatre with or which box he occupied."

She didn't believe the gentleman she'd seen to be one of the lost heirs. But who was she to deny His Grace and Lady March their hope?

"Do you recall anything else?"

"I'm sorry, Picus. It all happened so quickly."

"Please do not worry yourself, Miss Teverton." He offered a slight bow. "I will see what can be discovered. Enjoy your day."

"Thank you, Picus."

Rays of sunlight pushed through the morning haze signaling the start of yet another day in London, and still there was no sign of his brother. Maximus rubbed his eyes before running his hands through his hair. He was exhausted, frustrated, and beside himself. He'd spent half the night looking for Lucius, and the other half pacing and waiting for one of the footmen he'd sent out to return.

Where the bloody hell was his twin?

They'd only been in London a few days and already there was a significant change in his brother, and not a good one. His brother was on a downward spiral and there was nothing he could do to change the descension into a less than desirable world.

Soft footsteps signaled he was not alone. He turned around and looked into a pair of deep brown eyes weighed down with worry. "Any word?" Larentia's voice cracked. "He doesn't know anyone. Where could he have gone?" She stepped further into the drawing room, pulling her shawl tighter about her shoulders.

You didn't have to know someone to get into trouble, but he wasn't about to share his opinion with

Larentia. Instead, he tried to put her mind at ease. "I'm sure Lucius isn't in any danger." *Yet.* "Why don't you get some rest? I'll inform you the moment I receive news."

Larentia sucked in a long deep breath, and then simply nodded her acquiescence. Maximus knew she was beyond exhaustion with concern to relent so quickly without so much as a word. She trudged from the room leaving him alone with his thoughts once again.

Damn his brother. The older Lucius got, the more inconsiderate of their adoptive mother he became. He glanced at the clock on the mantle. He'd give the footman fifteen more minutes before he...

A cheerful whistle followed by the front door closing drifted up into the drawing room. Storming toward the sound, Maximus met Lucius as he reached the first floor.

"Where have you been?"

"Enjoying the city." Lucius's nonchalance did not sit well with Maximus.

"Do you have any idea how much you worried Larentia?" his demand thundered through the room.

"There wasn't anything to worry about. I simply wanted to taste the delights of the city, and—"

"And bring ruin upon yourself." Maximus narrowed his gaze, looking directly at his brother. "Damn it Lucius, everything we are, everything we have, is because of Larentia and Grandfather."

"I don't have to answer to anybody, especially not you. We're the same age or have you forgotten? I'm a grown man—"

"Damn it, then start acting like it." The words rumbled from Maximus's mouth, startling his brother. Wide unfathomable eyes settled on him. *Bloody hell.* He needed to change tactics, finding some middle ground. Softening his tone, Maximus continued, "I don't want to argue. There have been a lot of changes as of late, and Larentia is still grieving Grandfather's death. If nothing else, rein in those desires, for her sake."

Lucius's features sagged with remorse. "For Larentia's sake, I will. And I'll even find a way to make amends." He took in a sharp breath. "But don't expect my good behavior to last for long."

It never did.

After a rather tumultuous morning, Maximus wanted to be left alone with his thoughts, and what better way than to spend the afternoon outdoors on a pleasant Spring day. Since a horse was not at his disposal, a long walk would have to suffice.

"Going somewhere without me?" Lucius called as he strolled down the stairs with Larentia at his side.

"Like I could ever escape you," Maximus cautiously teased.

"I'm afraid we're bound together for life, my dear brother." Humor lingered on his words. It seemed as if Lucius was somewhat back to normal—or what passed for normal since their Grandfather's passing—after this morning's incident. At the very least, Lucius was attempting to make amends with Larentia.

"I'm going for a walk. Care to join me?" Maximus offered.

"That would be lovely. Lucius and I had the same idea." And without further ado, the trio alighted to the foyer.

Before too long they were strolling along the footpath toward Kensington Gardens. It was nearing the fashionable hour when it would seem that all of London wanted to see and be seen. Chatter and giggles trumped the sounds of nature, making it nigh impossible to enjoy the outing. His plan for a pleasant walk had been thwarted. Maximus made a mental note to avoid this time of day in the future.

Even Larentia seemed lost in her own thoughts, while Lucius strutted down the path like a peacock fanning its feathers for all to admire. And because they were identical twins, Maximus was unwillingly put on display as well.

"Do you not ever tire of being stared at?"

"No," Lucius said as he smiled at the passing ladies. "You should follow suit and enjoy being seen. Looks are a fleeting luxury and I intend to take full advantage of mine while I have them."

Their good looks might have proven an asset on many occasions, especially while traveling on the Continent, but Maximus wanted more from life than bedding beautiful women in various countries. He inhaled deeply and let out a long slow breath. He wanted so much more. He wanted...

The lady from the theatre. She was here.

In the near distance, the object of his thoughts was riding in a carriage. Loose strands of golden hair had escaped her bonnet, gently caressing her face. If he picked up his pace, he might be able to reach the conveyance. There was nothing inappropriate in offering a pleasant afternoon greeting.

"Oh, Larentia, must we hear about the history of the gardens?" Lucius's complaint distracted Maximus from his plan. "Can't we just enjoy the view?" he said as his gaze followed a pretty lady dressed in too much pink.

He was just about to excuse himself and go in search of the lady when Larentia opened and closed her mouth as if to respond to Lucius. Her brows drew together. She edged closer to Maximus and uttered, "I believe we're being followed."

"Don't be silly, Larentia," Lucius announced. "You thought someone was following us earlier when we were shopping, too."

She shifted her eyes to the right and then nodded in the same direction. "The handsome grey-haired gentleman has been strolling in the same direction as us since we arrived."

"There are plenty of people walking in the same direction," Maximus said, attempting to reassure Larentia and return to his original goal of finding the lady. He took a quick glance about. She was gone...again.

"I can't shake the feeling that someone is watching..." She stopped mid-sentence and turned her attention to Lucius. "Did you do something?"

"Why must you always assume I am in trouble?"

Not being able to resist, Maximus jumped in and teased, "In, created, stumbled upon—it's always the same, and always comes back to you, dear brother."

"I am completely innocent of any charges."

Larentia shot Lucius an incredulous glare. "If you say so."

"I do say so." He gave Maximus a sideways glance. "I've been restricted from engaging in any nefarious activities or private enjoyments with the opposite sex." Lucius brought a hand to his chest and declared, "I've been a perfect saint."

Perfect saint? Maximus had not realized his brother even knew the meaning of being virtuous. He wanted to add that it had not even been a full day since Lucius's last incident but thought better of it. They were having a pleasant afternoon and he didn't want to spoil it with an argument.

Shaking her head, a slight laugh lined Larentia's words. "You are quite the scoundrel Lucius."

"Not yet, but one can hope," Lucius said with a mischievous look and a wink. And that was precisely why Maximus took it upon himself to watch over his brother.

They continued along toward Kensington Gardens. Every so often, Maximus glanced over his shoulder to pacify Larentia's suspicion, but he did not espy anything unusual. Numerous couples were enjoying the fine day, the gray-haired man Larentia had noticed earlier was strolling casually in the distance looking up into the trees—presumably at birds, and several ladies giggled behind gloved hands. There was nothing out of the ordinary around them.

Before Maximus could offer further reassurances, a rather portly woman wearing a bright crimson hat almost as wide as she, scurried toward them. "Oh, my dearest Miss St. Albans. I heard you were in Town via Lady Kenton, and could hardly believe it, but here you are! And with your sons!"

"Good afternoon, Lady Craythorne. It is true, we're residing in London." Larentia introduced Maximus and Lucius, and as per usual, there was much commentary.

"You're both quite similar and quite handsome. I believe it shan't be too much trouble to find a wealthy heiress for each of you."

A horrified look crossed Larentia's features that bordered on comical. "They are not in the marriage mart quite yet, Lady Craythorne. We've only just arrived—"

"Not in the marriage mart, pshaw!" Lady Craythorne ended with a dismissal of her hand. "Whether they know it or not, all men are in search of a bride. That's why they come to Town." She shifted her attention to Maximus and Lucius. "And how are you enjoying London?"

"Very much—" Lucius began but was interrupted by yet another question.

"Have you been to the theatre?"

Maximus had the suspicion that Lady Craythorne did not let anyone finish a thought and rather enjoyed hearing herself speak. Of course, the pitch of her voice made it rather impossible for those within ten feet not to hear. However, he suspected her knowledge of the *ton* to be quite limitless. He still did not know how to go about discovering the identity of the lady he'd met last evening. Damn, he thought of nothing else. From the moment he'd held her in his arms, he'd wanted to know more about her. He'd never experienced such an instant attraction to a woman before.

"Lady Craythorne, perhaps you could solve a slight mystery for me?"

Eyes wide, she leaned forward intently. "Of course."

Maximus kept his tone low with the hope Lady Craythorne would follow suit. "There was a lady—"

"You didn't tell me you met a willing woman," Lucius jested.

Maximus narrowed his eyes and shot his brother a glare before continuing, "As I was saying, I left our box to stretch my legs. And happened across a lady. She had the most remarkable eyes—one green and one brown."

At the mention of the eyes, Lady Craythorne inhaled quickly, "Oh, you must be referring to Miss Teverton. I have never known it even possible to have two different-colored eyes, but she is proof." The spot between her dark brows narrowed. "She rarely comes to Town however, and has been firmly on the shelf for quite a few years now."

On the shelf? The woman he encountered could not be that old, and certainly not a spinster. Perhaps Lady Craythorne had her gossip confused. Maximus attempted to ask another question but before he could formulate a sentence, Lady Craythorne veered off on another tangent about an Italian actress and the nephew of a duke.

At the very least he knew she wasn't married, and now was in possession of a name. *Miss Teverton.*

After a couple of wet days, Maximus was aching for exercise. He was not used to being cooped up inside with nothing to do. He missed the country, missed riding, missed tending to the land, but most of all, he missed his grandfather. On days such as this, they would spend hours in the library, researching, discovering, sharing. At least his mind would have been stimulated. The library at their London townhouse was lacking at best with only a handful of books, most of which on poetry.

Maximus followed Lucius into the sparse space. Larentia had told them the room had once been reserved for her great aunt's collection of porcelain animal figurines, which had ranged in size from quite small and dainty to life size. Thankfully, those items had been removed years ago and, until Larentia made other plans, the room was ideal for what the brothers had in mind.

"Ready to try your luck again?" Lucius taunted Maximus as he took off his shirt and tossed it on the wooden floor, then stretched his fingers.

"It does not take luck to best you, but skill, my dear brother." Maximus tossed his shirt on top of his brother's. "As I've proven many times in the past."

A heavy exaggerated sigh rushed from Lucius's mouth. "You're not going to bring up the horse races again, are you?"

"Of course not. Why would I mention your lack of riding—"

"Ho there, that's enough." Lucius raised his fists. "Just because you've won every race doesn't—"

"Not to mention stayed on the horse for an entire race."

"A minor technicality." Lucius jabbed with his right arm. "Come on. Enough chatter. Are you ready?"

"I believe I am up to the challenge of besting you again," Maximus teased as he took his stance. At least in this arena, they were equally skilled, but he wasn't about to admit that to his brother.

Lucius stretched his arms wide several times before hopping from side to side.

"Are you going to dance around with fancy footwork or engage?" Maximus jeered.

"Fancy footwork? I think you'll change your words once my fist makes contact with you." Lucius extended his arm with short jabs. They sparred for several minutes before Lucius began with the inevitable siege of questions that always were par for the course during their fights. "Why didn't other relatives search for us?"

Since they were adolescents, it seemed the only time the two brothers had felt completely at ease expressing themselves—even though they always seemed to know what the other was thinking but rarely spoke of it—had been while boxing.

Lucius had asked that question more times than Maximus could remember. He had often pondered the very same one and always reasoned through the possibilities. "Perhaps there weren't others." He attempted to change the subject. "Did you read your letter from Grandfather yet?"

"No." Lucius shifted his weight and the topic he'd been avoiding since their grandfather passed away. "What about our mother?"

"She could have died in childbirth." Their father had died protecting them, that much they had known.

Lucius dropped his hands. "You always have an answer, don't you?"

He let out a long sigh. "It had always been easier to not think about who she might have been, and besides, Larentia and Grandfather gave us an exceptional life. I would rather focus on the good, rather than the why or why nots."

Lucius raised his fist and started prancing back and forth. "Aren't you curious?"

Maximus swung his own fist, narrowly missing Lucius's jaw. "No." It had taken years to bury that curiosity and he did not want to think about the what-ifs.

"Remember the rules, gentlemen," Larentia said as she entered the room, her brown hair streaked with silver shimmered in the rays of sunlight now cascading into the empty space. "I still don't understand why it is so appealing to try and prove your manliness in such a barbaric way."

"Would you rather it be swords at dawn?"

"Or perhaps pistols?" Maximus added with a wink.

"Not amusing. And both of you well know that I'm a better shot than either of you."

When the day had come for Grandfather to teach the boys how to handle a pistol, Larentia had insisted on being present for fear one—or possibly all three— had got into trouble. Much to everyone's surprise, and Grandfather's delight, Larentia had proved to be quite proficient with a gun.

She strolled further into the room, lines of concentration deep along her brows.

Maximus dropped his fists. "What's wrong?"

"Along with Lady Kenton, we've received an invitation to dine with The Duke of Warrington and The Dowager Marchioness of March."

"Seems like quite an illustrious pair." Lucius took the words right out of Maximus's mouth. "Why did *we* receive an invitation?"

"Honestly, I have not a clue." Larentia picked up their shirts and tossed them to them. "Perhaps Lady Kenton thought to introduce us to those in her circle and..." Her words died off as she whipped around. She eyed them both before she began her interrogation. "Neither of you have been engaging in something you shouldn't, have you?"

"And by neither of us, do you mean me?" Lucius teased, before turning serious. "No, I have not done anything, Larentia."

Maximus took the invitation card from Larentia's hand and read through it. "Lady Kenton's influence must be the reason for this request. There could be no other..." He paused as a thought came to mind. "Do you believe Grandfather could have been acquainted with His Grace?"

"He did dictate numerous letters each month, but I don't remember one to the Duke of Warrington." Although illness had weakened his body, Grandfather's mind had remained sharp till the end. He had taken great pride in keeping up with his correspondences until the pain had become unbearable. A slight laugh, followed by a heavy sigh escaped Larentia's lips. "I do miss him."

Maximus strolled up to Larentia, Lucius right behind him, and brought his surrogate mother into his embrace. "We miss him too, but you have us."

A sad sort of smile crossed her face. "I know, but someday even the two of you will marry and then—"

"We will never desert you," Lucius said as he placed a kiss on the top of Larentia's head.

"We will always take care of you," Maximus added. "You are the only family we have, and even if we marry into the largest family in all of England, you are still *our* family, and always will be, nothing can change that."

The sadness lingered for just a moment before the full weight of their words seemed to absorb into her thoughts. "Thank you." She tightened her hold on Maximus as if afraid he would be snatched from her. "Sometimes I do wonder if Father and I did you a disservice by not training you for an occupation."

"Let's not focus on that topic again." Maximus did not want to think about the future at the moment. "You said it yourself, something will come to fruition and until then we will enjoy the city."

"And dine with a duke."

Chapter Three

IF IT HADN'T been for Lady Kenton's occasional comment about the pleasant weather London was now experiencing after the rain, the ride to The Duke of Warrington's residence in Mayfair would have passed in silence. It wasn't every day that the daughter of a baron, accompanied by her two adopted sons of unknown lineage, were invited to dine by such an esteemed peer.

As the carriage slowed to a gentle stop, Maximus peered through the window. On the outside, His Grace's residence was everything he'd imagined it would be—grand and impressive, stark and uninviting. Dread settled into his gut. What on earth were he and Lucius doing here? He glanced over at his brother who was shaking his head, brows drawn together, and knew his twin was wondering the same.

However, the moment they entered the illustrious townhouse, they were treated as esteemed guests. Servants in red and gold livery bustled about their duties, each staring inquisitively at their party as they were escorted into the grand foyer. Even Lady Kenton was silent. Everything about this household was larger than life and on such a grand scale. Not that the home they'd shared with Larentia and Grandfather was paltry—Grandfather had been a baron after all. This residence was palatial, extravagant, exquisite, and...impersonal. There was no sense of who lived here. It was just a place to reside when in Town.

Before Maximus could formulate an opinion about everything surrounding them and why *they* were here, a tall, thin gentleman approached. His crest of hair was completely white, a stark contrast to his dark brown eyes. He looked vaguely familiar. *Where have I seen him before?* He searched his memory looking for answers.

"Thank you for accepting the invitation, Lady Kenton, Miss St. Albans. You may call me Picus, I am His Grace's assistant." His greeting was warm and friendly, and nothing that should alarm them. "And these are?"

"My adopted sons, Mr. Maximus St. Albans and Mr. Lucius St. Albans."

"Good evening, gentlemen. I must say it is a pleasure to make your acquaintance," his voice brimmed with excitement.

Maximus thought Picus's greeting far too enthusiastic. Why would meeting him and his brother garner such a reaction? Picus then went on to eye Maximus from top to bottom, before shifting his gaze and performing the same inspection of Lucius. Maximus was certain a comment about their identical appearance would be forthcoming, but much to his astonishment, the man held his tongue.

Lucius eyed Maximus. He could practically read his brother's thought—*What the bloody hell is this all about?*

"His Grace and Lady March are waiting in the gold parlor." Picus did not wait for a response but ushered their party toward an impressive hall lined with large paintings.

Except for the soft cadence of their footsteps, they followed in silence. Maximus admired canvas after canvas of what looked like the Italian countryside. But there was one in particular that caught his attention. He stopped in front of a painting of the Temple of Vesta. The rotund structure with a columned portico set against a clear blue sky reminded him of his time in Rome. Exploring ancient ruins ravaged by time and neglect had been part of his daily routine while visiting The Eternal City.

"This way, please," Picus called to Maximus, bringing him back to the present.

The moment they walked into the parlor, all eyes turned toward them. Maximus followed behind Larentia, but came to an abrupt halt when he saw the woman who had been plaguing his thoughts for the past several days. *Miss Teverton.* What was she doing here? As their eyes met, shock jolted his body. However, she did not appear surprised to see him.

"Oh my!" A woman seated beside an older gentleman gasped, disrupting Maximus's thoughts. Despite being clad in black, her appearance was elegant, regal.

The older man—presumably His Grace—patted the woman's hand gently but said nothing. Maximus continued to stare at him. He looked like an older version of himself. Surely his eyes must be deceiving him. Confusion, uncertainty, and curiosity wrestled in his mind, colliding with a surge of unnamed emotions.

"Your Grace, you're already acquainted with Lady Kenton. This is Miss St. Albans, and Mr. Maximus St. Albans, and Mr. Lucius St. Albans," Picus introduced them, then took a step back and said no more.

Silence engulfed the room as all parties just stared at each other.

His Grace stood and strolled toward them, his gaze never wavering. "You're probably wondering why Lady March and I asked you here." His tone was cautious. "I only have one question for you, Miss St. Albans, at this time. How did these two men come to be in your care?"

Lady Kenton looked at Larentia, who glanced at Maximus, who looked over at his brother, who was looking back at him. He knew Lucius was thinking the same thing. This is all very odd.

Larentia swallowed hard. "Your Grace, I do not understand why we were invited here today, but I will share with you the events which brought Maximus and Lucius into my care." She paused a moment and, in a fashion only she could do, questioned His Grace. "And in turn, I hope you will explain why you're so interested in my adopted sons?"

"Yes, of course, I mean no disrespect," His Grace quickly reassured in a pleasant tone. "Thank you for your cooperation, Miss St. Albans."

Larentia held her head high and related the tale the brothers had heard so many times over the years. She'd never tried to hide their identity or withhold anything she knew. She was the most honest person they'd ever known, so it was of great concern that she was now being questioned, especially about them.

Unspoken protectiveness passed between the brothers as they stepped forward and flanked Larentia, offering support as she spoke. "Twenty-three years ago, I was in London and—"

"I don't mean to interrupt, Miss St. Albans, just as you're beginning to explain," Lady March stood and began to apologize, "but do you happen to recall the exact date?"

"As a matter of fact, I do. My great aunt passed away on the fourteenth of April in the year seventeen ninety-six. Anxious to see my father again, I left London a day later. Travel was made slow by the weather. I was within a quarter day's journey from my home near Plymouth when we lost a wheel. That was on the twenty-first of April."

The Duke edged forward, making direct eye contact with Larentia, as he questioned, "Are you absolutely sure of the dates?"

"Yes, quite sure, Your Grace."

His Grace gave Lady March a curious look before he encouraged Larentia to finish her story. And through it all, Miss Teverton sat perfectly still, her eyes glazed and features grimacing, as if remembering something painful, and yet, she was still the most beautiful, intriguing creature Maximus had ever seen.

In a matter-of-fact tone, Larentia continued to relay the story of how the twins became part of her family. "The weather cleared, and since the late afternoon sun still provided ample light, I decided to take a walk while my driver and coachman repaired the wheel. I heard babies crying and thought it odd, considering there was no village or homes nearby. I followed the sound and discovered the boys firmly held in the arms of a man who was clinging to life. I asked his name. He mumbled incoherent words before saying, 'Protect the babies.' I asked his name again. He fought for air, before murmuring, 'Malvagio.' He died moments later before saying anything else."

"Oh my," Lady March gasped prompting Miss Teverton to join her side. "Were the children injured?"

"No, just hungry. My coachman searched the man. He had several stab wounds and a large gash on his leg that smelled putrid. The surrounding area held no clue as to what might have happened. Except for the name he gave, there was nothing to identify him. I took the children home with me, hired Lupa, a wet nurse from my village, and tried for many years to find information regarding anyone with the name Malvagio, but to no avail. My father was Baron St. Albans and together we brought up the boys. They were educated and cared for as if they were our own kin." Her voice cracked on the last word but still she carried on with her story. "Four years ago, my father sent them on the Grand Tour, but their time was cut short by his illness. They returned home and helped me care for him. My father passed away last Michaelmas." Although Larentia's voice was filled with emotion, she held her composure.

"Oh, I am sorry for your loss, Miss St. Albans," Lady March offered with true sincerity.

Uncomfortable seconds passed while they waited for someone, anyone, to say something. Maximus took

Larentia's cold hand in his and whispered, "Are you alright?"

Larentia did not answer, but simply nodded.

On the contrary, Lady March seemed quite overcome with emotion. She wiped a tear from her eye as she whispered something to Miss Teverton.

A soft gasp escaped Miss Teverton's lips as wide, surprised eyes settled directly on him.

After several more minutes, His Grace finally addressed their curious party. "And now it is my turn to explain." There was a moment's pause as he seemed to gather his thoughts and emotions. "Twenty-three years ago, this past April, my twin grandsons were stolen from us here in London. The Marquess of March, my late son, searched and searched for his sons, but never found them, or discovered why they were taken."

"We never gave up looking for them," Lady March interjected, raw emotion rendering her features stricken. "But when my husband died unexpectedly, the pain became so unbearable." She brought a trembling hand to her lips. "I apologize..."

Miss Teverton took Lady March's other hand in hers and rubbed it gently. Indiscernible words passed between Miss Teverton and Lady March. *Is she Lady March's companion?*

His Grace's eyes were clouded with the sadness of a parent who'd lost a child and endured much tragedy. "My other son assumed the title of Marquess and continued the search for his nephews."

Maximus squeezed Larentia's hand. "What does this have to do with my brother and me? You can't possibly believe we're the missing twins?"

His Grace paced back and forth for a brief moment before explaining, "Through the years, many have tried to deceive us, to claim they were our lost boys, but each time, they were discovered to be frauds. You did not come to us with claims of lineage, *we* asked you to come here. Miss Teverton mentioned your resemblance to one of my nephew's sons. Picus instantly saw the similarity to my Martin."

Maximus suddenly realized why the man looked so familiar. "You've been following us."

"Yes. I apologize if I caused any concern, but after so many years of searching and much disappointment, I needed to verify your intentions for myself before raising His Grace's hopes once again."

"Intentions?" Maximus could feel the anger bubbling within. "We have no *intentions*. Miss St. Albans has not lied and—"

"Maximus, please," Larentia whispered. "I don't believe His Grace, Lady March, or Picus meant any disrespect."

Lady Kenton gasped as if the situation just dawned on her. She glanced from one brother to the other. "I hadn't realized before, but my goodness, they do look much like the late Marquess."

Whispers and chatter swirled about. They couldn't possibly believe Maximus and Lucius were the lost heirs, could they?

As if sensing the direction of Maximus's thoughts, His Grace questioned, "How do we know if they are truly our boys?"

"I wish there was a way to know." Lady March's words hung in the air as if they were independent from her body.

"There must be a way," Picus said as he continued to stare at Maximus and Lucius.

And still through it all, Miss Teverton remained utterly still, jaw tight, eyes glassy and fixed on some distant time or place.

Larentia sucked in a deep breath, turned to Maximus and then to Lucius. "There is a way to settle this." Maximus could feel her bravado weakening. She turned her attention back to His Grace and Lady March. "Everything I have told you is true, but perhaps there is something..."

"What proof could you offer?" The words rushed from His Grace's mouth, lined with hope.

All eyes settled on Larentia, waiting for her next words. "This may seem quite unorthodox and unacceptable under normal conditions."

"This entire situation has been anything but normal, Miss St. Albans." His Grace's voice softened. "Please continue."

"If you would allow the boys to remove their coats and cravats, this may be settled within a matter of moments."

The Duke nodded his head, and with keen interest, watched Maximus and his brother take off the aforementioned clothing. Out of the corner of his eye he spied Miss Teverton worrying her bottom lip, while watching intently.

"When I found the babies, I was amazed at how similar they were in appearance." Larentia took in a deep breath, her strength unwavering. "They even had matching birthmarks."

With the mention of the word, both Maximus and Lucius pulled the collars of their shirts wide to reveal their birthmarks, light brown in color and in the shape of what looked like a crescent moon.

"Oh my," Lady March's soft gasp drifted across the room and settled in Maximus's chest. Could this woman be his mother? Could they be the grandsons of a duke?

"You are my sons!" Lady March choked on her words as tears streamed down her cheeks. Then she rushed over to the boys. She stared at each birthmark for a moment, before bringing a shaky hand, to first Lucius's cheek then to Maximus's. "I thought I would never see you again."

His thoughts scrambled to understand. The seventh Duke of Warrington was *his* grandfather? His mother was alive and had been searching for them all these years?

Larentia began to step away, but Maximus grasped her hand in a silent plea, begging her to stay. He was not going to lose her. She was his family and even if what His Grace and Lady March said was true, he was not going to cast Larentia aside.

His Grace approached the boys with joyous caution. "Are they really our Zachary and Richard?"

"Yes," Lady March cried. "They have the same birthmark as their father."

Father. That word was so foreign to him. Maximus had always believed his father had died protecting them. *Then who was the man Malvagio?*

Lady March stepped away, allowing His Grace a closer look. He stared intently at each of the twins for countless seconds before bringing them within the folds of his arms. His words were laced with so much emotion. "My grandsons have returned home." As he released them, his whole face spread into a smile. "This truly is a joyous day! You will reside here, and we will host a grand ball to announce your return."

Out of the corner of his eye, Maximus saw Larentia slip further away from them. His world was spinning out of control. The faces around him became transparent as his thoughts settled on one person. Grandson of a duke or not, he was not going to abandon Larentia.

"I'm sorry, Your Grace," he began as he stepped back, "but I will not leave Miss St. Albans."

"Nor will I," Lucius chimed in. Knowingness passed between them. They might have their differences at times, but when it mattered, Maximus and Lucius were one.

"You are my heirs," disappointment weighed heavy in His Grace's words.

Lady March intervened, "I know this must be quite a shock, but we've searched for so long..." Her words trailed as tears began anew.

Miss Teverton rushed to her side. "Give them time," she soothed.

"Time? Twenty-three years have already been wasted," His Grace's voice filled the room, not with anger, but with frustration and remorse. "I'm not getting any younger. I want to know my grandsons. They have to..."

"Warrington," Miss Teverton said with firmness. *Was she His Grace's mistress?* The thought soured in his stomach. "Getting upset and making demands is not going to make this easier on anyone."

On a long exhale, His Grace's shoulders sagged. He shook his head several times before addressing Miss Teverton. "You're right, my dear. What are we to do?"

My dear?

Grandfather or not, Maximus had the sudden urge to punch the man in the face.

Placing a hand on His Grace's other arm, Lady March said, "A word, please." She turned to Miss Teverton. "Sabina, would you please join us." The trio left the room, followed by Picus, leaving everyone else to wonder what would happen next.

Chapter Four

WHAT COULD HIS Grace, Lady March—no, they were actually his grandfather and mother, and Miss Teverton possibly need to discuss?

Numerous silent minutes passed before Lady Kenton turned to Larentia, and questioned, "Did you have any clue your sons were related to a duke?"

A long heavy sigh escaped Larentia's lips. "They're not my sons. They're the sons of a marquess." She looked from one brother to the other. "Please know, I never suspected your true heritage."

"I...we know, but..." Lucius said as he took her hand.

"But we're not leaving you," Maximus finished his brother's sentence.

"Nor will you have to," His Grace said as he returned with Lady March and Miss Teverton at his side.

Silence enveloped the room as they waited to hear the fate of their future.

Lady March approached, her eyes softened as she began to speak, "My companion is much wiser than Warrington or myself, and has suggested a possible solution to this conundrum."

Relief coursed through Maximus's veins when he heard the word 'companion', but his mind was still swirling with all the information that had just been revealed.

"Of course, I know what it is like to lose children. Miss St. Albans, you obviously care a great deal for your adopted sons and they in turn for you." Lady

March went to Larentia's side. "Their fates could have been far worse. I will be forever grateful for what you did. More grateful than you can possibly imagine. You will always have a place in our home, alongside my sons."

It took a moment for Maximus to realize what Lady March was offering. *No, they couldn't...* He must have misunderstood. "You want Larentia to live with you?"

"Yes. Warrington and I are in agreement." Lady March turned to Larentia. "We want you to join our household, alongside Maximus and Lucius." It was odd to hear Lady March use their given names. They'd only just met. Maximus sighed inwardly. No, they hadn't just *met*, they'd just been reunited with their mother, their grandfather...their family.

Larentia worried her hands as she spoke, "I couldn't possibly. It is quite out of the ordinary."

"As I said earlier, this situation is anything but normal." His Grace stepped forward, looking directly at Larentia, his words sincere. "We insist. You took on the burden of rearing these two as if they were your own, and for that, we shall be forever indebted to you."

"Please say you will agree," Maximus said. "I..." He glanced over at Lucius. "We cannot accept without you."

A gentle hand cupped his cheek. Larentia smiled brightly. She whispered with obvious feeling, "You and Lucius have been my greatest joy. I will consider the invitation."

This conversation was far from over.

"Wonderful. Now that's settled, we must begin to make arrangements for..." His Grace's words trailed off. The spot between his brows crinkled with confusion. "We don't know who Zachary is, and who is Richard."

Lady March's head whipped around, her features full of concern. "Oh dear, we don't." She turned to Larentia. "Was there any mention...anything that would give us an idea of who is who? What were they were wearing when you discovered them?"

"I apologize Lady March, but they were dressed in identical outfits. If you would like to see them—"

"You saved them?"

"Yes. I saved everything, and I kept a journal of all their accomplishments."

"A journal..." Lady March choked on her words. "About my sons?"

"Yes. I recorded everything from the day they first crawled to when they left for the Grand Tour."

Lady March began to cry again. "I apologize. I never dreamed that..." Once again Miss Teverton went to her side, comforted her.

The compassion Miss Teverton showed for Lady March touched Maximus's soul. They appeared to be very close. Dozens of questions stormed his mind. How long had she been Lady March's companion? Were His Grace and Lady March in the box that evening?

"But that still doesn't answer the question as to who is the elder," Picus stated.

Maximus's thoughts once again were being pulled from Miss Teverton. The topic of who was older had always been a source of contention and argument between the brothers for as long as he could remember. They would jest about it, especially when Maximus was lecturing his brother about something he shouldn't be doing, but this conundrum went beyond any simple argument about who should listen to whom.

"We can deal with that issue in the coming weeks. What's most important is my grandsons have been reunited with us." His Grace clasped his hands together. "First, we must begin preparations to announce their homecoming, then we leave for Warrington Hall and the annual house party. There is truly a reason to celebrate this year."

Not for the first time since their arrival, Maximus's head was spinning. "What...what do you mean leave?"

"You and your brother are my heirs. You currently know nothing of your family. My boys, you are the grandsons of the Duke of Warrington." Pride resounded in his words. "With that comes responsibility, a responsibility to know your heritage and prepare you for your future."

Tension coursed through his veins as Maximus felt his freedom being stripped away. In the span of a couple of hours, he and Lucius had gone from being orphaned children of unknown origin, to the grandsons of the seventh Duke of Warrington, and one of them was destined to be the eighth. It was a future he was unsure he wanted.

Lady March stepped forward, clearly realizing his struggle. "I know this is all very sudden for you both, all three of you in fact." She looked over to Larentia. "But we have been searching for so long, never giving up hope that someday we would discover your whereabouts, and all we want is some time, time to get know one another." She looked over toward His Grace, some sort of understanding passing between them.

His Grace turned and addressed Larentia. "We will give you three a moment. Picus will wait in the hall. When you're ready, he will see you to the Florentine drawing room." Lady Kenton followed His Grace, Lady March, and Miss Teverton, leaving Maximus and Lucius alone with Larentia.

Maximus watched Larentia trudge toward the window as even more questions and conflicting thoughts swirled in his mind, and yet the one that kept coming to the forefront was how was this affecting Larentia?

She was the only mother they'd ever known. She'd cared for them, nurtured them, loved them unconditionally as if they were her kin. And now, she stood perfectly still, gazing out the window, creating distance.

The only time Maximus could recall having seen her like this was when her father had died. It had always been difficult for Larentia to express emotion, and today was no exception.

Lucius leaned in and uttered, "What do you think is bothering her?"

"Are you that insensitive?" The words rumbled from Maximus's mouth. "I am shocked you even have to ask."

"She knows we care for her, and besides, you heard our mother, Larentia will always be welcome here. We don't have to worry about Larentia and we're set for life."

It was amazing how easily Lucius accepted his new life, and shocking how willing he was to give up everything that had been important to them just that morning. He wanted to argue with his brother, talk some sense into Lucius, but now was not the time. He wanted to ensure Larentia was alright.

"I'm going to join the others." Lucius spun around and strolled casually away as if this was the life he was meant to lead, the life he'd always known.

Maximus watched his twin leave the room, the rift between them widening. He would deal with Lucius later. Right now, Larentia needed him. Her perfect composure could not hide the sorrow marring her features. For the first time, she looked her fifty-five years.

"I will be making arrangements tomorrow to have your and Lucius's things taken to His Grace's residence." Her tone was matter-of-fact, but her eyes, her loving brown eyes, told a different story.

"And do I not have a say in my future?"

A sad smile teased her lips. "Not when you're the grandson of a duke, and his heirs."

Maximus went to Larentia and brought her into his embrace. Her shoulders sagged as her body heaved and tears flowed. Tears that tore at his insides.

It was the first time in his life he'd seen her cry. Not even when her father died had she shed a tear, claiming she was too relieved he was no longer suffering to be sorry he was no longer of this earth.

"I will not go. Not without you." Maximus could not leave her, not like this, not alone with no family. "Lucius can be the Duke's heir."

Larentia pulled away but gripped the edge of his coat. Her caring deep brown eyes held such love for him and Lucius. He could see her struggle, the argument lingering on the edge of her lips. "You—"

"You are my family," he stated before she could finish her reply. "You are the only mother I've known..." His words trailed off as something he'd never thought of before entered his mind. "Why did you never allow Lucius and me to call you Mother?"

She sniffled back the tears. "When you were little, I waited in dreadful anticipation for your real mother to come and take you away. I thought if I denied myself that title, it would be easier." Tears streamed down her face anew, and she wiped them away with a shaky hand. "Clearly, I was wrong," she said with a chuckle as she wiped the other side of her face.

"Larentia, I will never abandon you."

She gazed into his eyes, her features softening. "I cannot expect you to remain with me, to keep you from the life you were destined to live."

"Then you must accept the invitation given and come with us. I can't do this alone."

"I don't know." The words exited her mouth on a slow exhale.

A long silence passed between them before Maximus remembered the one thing he knew would change her mind.

"Do you remember that day when Grandfather sent you from his room, saying he needed to speak to Lucius and me?"

She nodded her head. "Yes, it was the last day he was truly coherent. He suffered so much after that. I hated seeing him in so much pain, the life slowly draining from him."

"I made a promise to him." Maximus took Larentia's hand within his and looked into her eyes, holding her gaze. "Grandfather needed to know his only child would be cared for. He loved you so much." He fought to maintain his composure as the words cracked in his throat. "I promised Grandfather that I would always take care of you. Please do not force me to break that promise."

Seconds lingered. He could sense her struggle but was relieved when she finally spoke. "I will accept, but if I am ever not needed—"

Maximus brought her back within his embrace. "My dearest Larentia, you will always be needed."

Sabina followed Warrington and Sylvia to the Florentine drawing room, barely hearing a word. She was still trying to come to terms with the fact that the man she'd collided with at the theatre was one of the lost heirs. For heaven's sake, she remembered the day they were born! She'd been seven years old and had waited with great anticipation to see the new babies.

Oh dear. She was *seven* years older than him.

It wasn't as if she truly believed Mr. St. Albans—or rather Lord Maximus, as he would now be referred to— would have ever pursued her, but the butterflies...oh, the delicious butterflies that filled her insides at just the thought of him made that dream an exquisite luxury. She hadn't felt this way...ever.

A long sigh escaped her lips. Better to let reality be her guide.

"Anything the matter, Sabina?" Sylvia questioned.

She would not diminish her friends joy with her own insecurities. She pasted on a smile. "Nothing at all. It's been quite the afternoon."

Warrington positively gleamed with pride. "It certainly has. I haven't been this happy since...well, since the day those boys were born." He turned to Sylvia. "After years of wondering and hoping, we can rest assured."

They strolled into the ornate Florentine drawing room, relaxing near the white marble fireplace. With the return of the twins there would be a lot of changes, not just for the twins, but her as well. Sabina's head began to hurt. What would happen to her? The cottage was still not ready. She couldn't possibly continue living with Sylvia and Warrington. Loneliness streaked across her horizon.

"I thought I would join you," an exuberant voice played against the walls.

Both Warrington and Sylvia broke into an open, friendly smile at the single brother who had entered the drawing room. Although they were twins, there was a distinct difference between the men Sabina couldn't quite name. However, one thing she knew for certain, with this one, there were no flutters in her stomach, no warmth in her cheeks. He must be Lord Lucius.

Thankfully he was not shy in solving the mystery for them. "I'm Lucius."

Sylvia let out a long sigh. "I'm sorry, I should..."

He shook his head, quickly reassuring Sylvia. "It's been twenty-three years. Even Larentia confuses us at times."

Sabina studied him. Both he and Lord Maximus stood tall and could command attention in any room they entered. Both were handsome beyond belief. Both had the Warrington piercing blue eyes. However, that's where the similarities faded. Lord Lucius knew he was in possession of all those things. He did indeed look exactly like his brother, but his manner was subtlety different. She'd noticed it when Miss St. Albans was telling her story, and when they were told they were the Duke's heirs. Lord Lucius had appeared over the moon, while Lord Maximus had been cautious with the news. And when Lord Maximus had expressed great concern for Miss St. Albans, Sabina's heart had practically melted.

She knew her brother cared for her, and Sylvia and Warrington had become like family to her, but she didn't believe anyone in the world cared for her the way Lord Maximus cared for his adoptive mother.

So lost in her own musings was she, all conversation drifted into an abyss. But the moment Lord Maximus entered the room, flutters flitted through her body, drawing her attention to him. Somehow her body knew the difference. *How was that even possible?*

As the conversation continued around her, Sabina heard none of it, too focused as she was on Lord Maximus. By the time dinner was called, all she really wanted was a quiet moment to contemplate all the events of the day. Sadly, one did not often get what one wanted.

Under normal circumstances, Sabina enjoyed the fare prepared by Warrington's London cook, but tonight she hardly tasted a morsel. Every time she glanced up from her meal, Lord Maximus's eyes were on her, warming her insides. It would all end once he discovered who she was, and her involvement twenty-three years ago.

The evening meal passed by pleasant measures, accompanied by stories about the late Marquess and his brother, Daniel, who was in Northumberland tending to estate business, and then the twins and their many escapades, and the home they kept with Miss St. Albans. Through it all, Sabina kept to herself. She was intrigued by Miss St. Albans. She must be close in age to Sylvia, and yet seemed content with spinsterhood, with herself. Perhaps she was thinking too hard about the situation. It certainly wouldn't be the first time. Perhaps she still could have a life full of purpose, just not the purpose she desired. If left to her own devices, Sabina could talk circles around herself all evening.

"What happened the night we were taken?" Lord Lucius asked in a cautious tone.

Oh dear. The question rattled her to the very core. Heat simmered within, threatening to boil her alive. Sabina clutched the table and fought to control her breath as the internal screaming threatened to consume her.

"Miss Teverton?" She heard her name crack through her thoughts but did not know who said it.

"Miss Teverton, are you alright?"

Heat rose within as the room began to spin, her heart pounding wildly in her chest, and yet all she could do was clutch the table.

"Sabina!"

The loud scream broke through the nightmare building in her mind. Her eyes flew open to find everyone staring at her with concern. The last thing she wanted to do was reveal the truth. She pushed away from the table.

"I...I'm feeling ill." She forced the hard lump in her throat down. "Please excuse me." Not waiting for acknowledgement, she pushed away from the table and scurried from the room as fast as her legs could take her.

Chapter Five

THE FOLLOWING DAY brought a whirlwind of activity. Decisions were being made with lightning speed, most of them without Maximus or Lucius's input. Before the sun had begun to dip into the horizon they were all ensconced at the Duke of Warrington's London residence attempting to adjust to their new life.

News of their discovery had already made the rounds in London several times over, each time with a slightly different variation. As they were shown to their perspective suites, Maximus could not help but wonder where Miss Teverton was hiding. Her behavior last night still puzzled him, and he was concerned for her. He believed the episode was more than just her feeling ill.

Retrieving several of his favorite books from the trunk, he organized them on the shelf. This task almost done. First, he would finish settling in, then inquire after her. However, his plan was disrupted by the arrival of Picus.

"Good afternoon, Lord..." Picus paused, clearly unsure which brother he was about to address. He couldn't fault the man, at least he did not make assumptions.

"Maximus."

"Thank you, my lord."

My lord. It sounded so foreign, and yet it was who he was now.

"Your grandfather is waiting in his study."

"Thank you." He followed Picus down several halls, eventually arriving at the drawing room, where Lucius was impatiently pacing.

"His Grace's study is at the far end of the hall, last door on the right." And with those final directions, Picus left the brothers.

Maximus did not know what to expect. He glanced over at Lucius as the brothers strolled side by side toward His Grace's study. "Nervous?"

"No." The single word spoke volumes. Lucius was only silent when nervous. Maximus sensed Lucius was just as anxious as he. Although his twin was embracing their new family with open arms, it still did not ease the anxiety of trying to assimilate into this world. Everyone was joyous that they had been found, yet neither knew what was expected of them.

They approached the open door with trepidation. Maximus glanced over to Lucius once again and whispered, "Do we knock?"

The answer came a moment later. "Come in, come in," His Grace said with enthusiasm. "I have been waiting all day for a moment to spend with my grandsons." His smile was warm and sincere.

His Grace glanced back and forth between Maximus and Lucius before commenting, "It is truly amazing how identical you both are in looks, but I suspect it ends there."

"Larentia always encouraged us to be our own person," Maximus said.

"That is quite admirable." His Grace strolled closer. "You are quite fond of Miss St. Albans." It wasn't a question, but a decisive statement.

"We owe her our life." No matter who they were or what titles they bore, they were the men they'd become because of her and Grandfather St. Albans.

"I cannot express enough how thankful I am that she is the one who discovered and cared for you both." His Grace turned and stared out the window for countless seconds before taking in a deep breath. On a long exhale he said, "I suppose you are wondering who will be the next Marquess of March." He whipped around and chuckled. "I have not a clue. Zachary was the elder, Richard born a few minutes later. At the time of birth, yarn was tied to Zachary's ankle, so we could tell you two apart. But now, we have no way of knowing. Until succession has been decided, you will be addressed as Lord Maximus and Lord Lucius respectively. You will each be given an allowance, have access to the best tailors in Town, and membership to my club."

How did one respond to such news? As recently as yesterday morning, Maximus had been anxious over his future, now he was being handed a living and admittance into London's most exclusive men's club. If he were being honest, he would have preferred an occupation where he could make a difference, or at least be useful.

Lucius, however, had no such qualms, and responded with enthusiasm. "Thank you, Your Grace."

His Grace clasped his hands behind his back and paced for a moment. "I realize that I am practically a stranger to you both, and perhaps this is too soon, but I'm not getting any younger, and..." He turned and faced them, his features softening. "It would give me great joy if you'd address me as 'Grandfather'."

Without hesitation Lucius once again leapt at the opportunity to assimilate into this environment and responded with great zeal, "Of course, Grandfather."

Maximus stared past His Grace into the flames dancing in the fireplace, unable to answer as recollections of the man who'd been his grandfather for twenty-three years rushed through his mind. Images of Grandfather St. Albans reading to him by the firelight, teaching him how to draw, talking to him about the world beyond England. His heart tore in half, struggling between accepting one life while seemingly betraying another.

His Grace must have sensed where his thoughts had strayed. "I spoke with Miss St. Albans earlier and she told me all of what her father did for you." He stepped closer. Only an arm's length separated them. "I have no intention of replacing his memory. I cannot change the past." His blue eyes, so similar to Maximus's own, were intense, sincere, and honest. "I only want the opportunity to create a future with my grandsons." Something familiar passed between them, a sense of connection. His Grace put a hand on Maximus's shoulder and squeezed gently. "You are so much like your father."

Maximus heard Lucius's sharp inhale and knew that harmless comment had struck at his brother's heart.

"Am I interrupting?" Lady March strolled in to the study, easing some of the tension now coursing between the brothers.

"No, my dear. I'm just getting to know our boys." The pride for his family filled the room.

It was a possessive statement, but somehow, Maximus was beginning to feel comforted by it. He was slowly becoming accustomed to the idea that these people were now his family. At no point had they asked Maximus and Lucius to renounce their past or hide their upbringing. Quite the contrary in fact.

Maximus's assessment was proven correct a moment later when Lady March occupied the brown leather chair near the fire and said, "Tell me about your upbringing. I want to hear every single detail."

Grandfather took the seat opposite her and motioned Maximus and Lucius to join them. They spent the next couple of hours sharing stories about when they were young, listened in turn to stories about their father and uncle, and just set about getting acquainted. Before too long, Maximus felt somewhat more at ease.

Lady March clasped her hands together. "As much as I would love to sit here all evening and hear more, we have Lady Shafton's soirée to ready ourselves for."

"I do enjoy soirées," Lucius said as he stood and offered his arm. "Allow me to escort you upstairs, Mother." Their mother's smile brightened the room at Lucius's use of her title.

Maximus knew exactly what Lucius was up to. He'd been hurt by their grandfather's innocent comment and wanted Maximus to pay. Lucius never liked coming in second to him.

Let him have his way. It's not worth the fight. He would not ruin the moment for their mother.

"I best be taking my leave as well," Grandfather stated as he joined Lucius.

Maximus watched the trio as they exited. He had a mother and a grandfather now. He loitered by the fire trying not to think. If he gave into all the thoughts, feelings, and emotions coursing through his body, he might never leave this spot.

Lucius was a fool to believe their lives would be an endless entertainment filled with unlimited funds and gaiety. He worried his brother would land himself in irreversible trouble one day quite soon.

"Oh, I'm sorry," Miss Teverton started as she entered the room. "I was looking for Lady March." The late afternoon sun glistened through the windows, settling on her creamy cheeks. "I will—"

"Please, don't go," the words rushed from his mouth. Maximus didn't want to be alone. And, truth be told, he had hoped to see her today.

Her eyes were gentle, understanding. "Is anything the matter?"

"No...yes...I..." Maximus ran a frustrated hand through his hair. He should be concentrating on trying to fit in, becoming more acquainted with his family, and yet with Miss Teverton in the room, his mind only wanted to think about her. He'd been formally introduced to her last night but hadn't had a moment to speak to her. He was curious about her place within the household, her friendship with his mother, and why on two previous occasions something had upset her.

She titled her head slightly and offered a knowing smile. "Might this have something to do with His Grace and Lady March and the new arrangements?"

"In part. You're quite perceptive."

"Not really. I'm just very acquainted with the situation and know how difficult this has been on everyone." Her tone held a degree of warmth and concern.

"Is that why you suggested the compromise with Miss St. Albans?"

"Yes. It is clear you care a great deal for her, and I know Lady March wants to spend as much time with you and Lord Lucius as she possibly can. It seemed the natural solution. I know from experience, Warrington and Lady March enjoy helping those in need."

"You're quite close to Lady March?"

"Yes." Admiration overflowed from the single word.

He thought about it for a moment. "When did you and my mother become friends?"

"I've known her all my life."

Maximus attempted to restrain himself from peppering her with questions, but to no avail. "Do you not have family?"

"I do, but I'm not close with my mother, and my sister-in-law dictates my brother's life." She inhaled deeply as she strolled toward the fireplace. She seemed to struggle with what she wanted to say.

"I don't mean to pry."

As she turned around, a sad sort of smile crossed her features before it was concealed. "Your mother has always been kind to me. After..." She paused, rethinking what she was about to say. "We were able to comfort one another."

Maximus suspected there was more to that comment but didn't want to press further at this time. "And you also knew my father?"

"Yes. Lord March and my father grew up together. Our country estates border one another." Miss Teverton's tone softened, sounding almost lighthearted. "I loved hearing all the tales of their adventures. They were quite mischievous from the stories I heard."

After His Grace's comment, he was curious. "What was he like?"

"Your father was a wonderful, caring person. He adored children and had been looking forward to the birth of his own." Sadness crept across her face once again. "After you were taken, Lord March did not rest. He was determined to find you and your brother. He suffered greatly. I'm sorry I cannot offer more. He died shortly after you and Lord Lucius were taken." Silence passed between them before she added, "You remind me of him."

"His Grace...I mean, my Grandfather said..." his words trailed off as he shook his head. "I'm sorry. I'm not used to—"

"There's no need to apologize. Warrington is a good and patient man. This will get easier with time. He is not expecting you to forget the family that raised you and your brother."

"I don't want to forget him." The confession rushed from his mouth, almost shocking him.

"Just because you've discovered you're the grandson of a duke does not diminish the role of your adopted grandfather." Miss Teverton was quickly becoming the voice of reason. "From all that I've heard, he *was* your grandfather. He cared for you and guided you."

"Thank you." Her kind, sincere words helped ease some of his current worries. "Will you be joining us at Lady Shafton's this evening?"

She replied with forced politeness. "No. Enjoy your evening Lord Maximus." And with those final words, she left the room and did not look back.

Miss Teverton was definitely a puzzle, one he definitely wanted the solution to.

A sennight later, the evening of the grand ball celebrating Maximus and Lucius's return had arrived and with it, a whole new set of anxieties. Maximus eyed his reflection once more. His new valet had turned his simple country style into something His Grace would no doubt approve and be proud of. He looked like he *was* the grandson of a duke.

With great trepidation, he left his room, but instead of joining his grandfather for a drink in his study, he sought the one person who could put his mind at ease.

Maximus raised his hand and was just about to knock when the door opened wide, startling both him and Larentia.

"Oh," Larentia clasped her hand to her chest. "I didn't expect to see you. I thought you would be with His Grace."

"I wanted to speak to you first." Maximus took in the sight of her. Larentia was positively radiant in aubergine. The color accentuated her brown hair and deep chocolate brown eyes. "You look lovely this evening."

"Thank you, but don't change the subject. What's troubling you?" Larentia had never coddled him, but the concern in her voice was palpable.

"It's all changing so fast. One moment, Lucius and I are unknowns, free to do as we please with little responsibility, and now..."

"You like responsibility," Larentia teased as she turned and closed her door.

"I feel like I'm losing my brother. Lucius has decided he likes the role of heir to a duke. He keeps vying for His Grace's attention. It has become a one-sided rivalry." Nothing soured his stomach faster than being at odds with his brother.

"And you?"

"I don't like all the attention. Everywhere we go, people stare."

"You're used to people staring."

"Because I'm an identical twin, not because I'm the long-lost grandson of a duke. It's different." How could he explain when he didn't understand himself?

"I know. Just give it time. Lady March and His Grace will help you both with this new life, and if nothing else, you can become a rake," she ended with a quip.

Maximus ignored her jest that under any other circumstance would have earned her a chuckle. "I'm just worried—"

"Stop worrying." She shook her head. "Stop worrying about being the grandson of a duke, about your brother, about me...about everything and just enjoy *this* evening." She looked over his attire and began to adjust his cravat. "It isn't every day that a duke announces the return of a marquess."

"It still has not been decided who will succeed His Grace."

"Time will tell. Come on, let's not keep the *ton* waiting."

Larentia took his offered arm and they strolled down the hall in silence. They'd just neared their destination when Maximus stated, "I expect you to save me a dance this evening."

"I don't dance." It was an age-old argument. Larentia had once confessed she used to enjoy dancing, but that was before she became a spinster, and decided spinsters did not partake in such amusements. Maximus hoped to change her mind.

It seemed as if all of London's upper echelon were attending this event. Several hundred guests had gathered and were now anxiously awaiting the appearance of the Duke of Warrington. Although it was common knowledge he would announce the legitimacy of Maximus and Lucius as the sons of his late heir, no one knew exactly what he would say. Ever since their discovery, rumors had swirled about what had happened all those years ago; who was eldest, who would be named the Marquess of March and the next Duke of Warrington, and why Lord Daniel—never mind the distance—still had not returned from Northumberland.

As His Grace, flanked by his two heirs, emerged on the balcony, all eyes turned upward, and conversation was reduced to a gentle hush of awe and anticipation. Seeing them so elegantly dressed, standing next to their grandfather, made Sabina's heart flutter. The family resemblance was quite astonishing. No one could deny that Lord Maximus and Lord Lucius were Warrington's kin. Behind the trio, standing in a place of honor were Lady March and Miss St. Albans.

Sabina had had the pleasure of conversing with Miss St. Albans on several occasions and was inspired by the woman's intelligence, knowledge, and determination to stay positive. She looked forward to becoming better acquainted with her, and knew they had a lot of common, both being firmly on the shelf and all.

Warrington gazed over the crowd from his perch on the balcony. Silence draped the grand ballroom as everyone waited for His Grace to speak.

"Twenty-three years ago, Lady March, my dearest daughter-in-law, gave my family the most precious gift of twin boys, but Fate would not allow us to revel in that joy before they were cruelly snatched from our lives. But even in her fickleness, Fate spared them a painful ending and delivered them safely into the hands of Miss St. Albans, who cared for and nurtured them. Through divine intervention, they have been returned to our family." Warrington paused, clearly emotional at having been reunited with his only grandchildren. "It is with great pleasure that I introduce my grandsons, Lord Maximus," he said as he waved a hand toward Maximus, who was dressed in deep navy, then toward his other grandson, who was clad in black, "And Lord Lucius."

The roar of applause echoed off every surface, filling every void. The missing heirs were finally home. Sabina sucked in a breath and said a silent prayer hoping the nightmare would end at last, and she too would have peace. *Please let the nightmare stop.*

A short time later, she watched as every eligible lady flirted with and swooned at the sight of the handsome twins as they mingled with their guests. A slight pang struck her heart. Those days had passed for her and she was most certainly a spinster now, no matter how many butterflies filled her stomach or how fast her heart raced when Lord Maximus was near. She couldn't complain though. Because of her brother and Sylvia, she had a good life, and plans for the future.

But sometimes the best laid plans were thrown from the carriage window at a high speed and trampled upon by every horse in the county. That was exactly how Sabina had felt the first time she'd met Lord Maximus at the theatre, although she hadn't known who he was at the time, and had no hopes for marriage. Despite what her mind knew for certain, her body continued to contradict every time Lord Maximus was near. For heaven's sake, she was a woman of thirty, not some love-sick debutante, but here she was all giddy inside as if this was her first season, hoping...no, praying someone would ask her to dance.

"Miss Teverton." The deep timbre of Lord Maximus's voice interrupted her thoughts.

"Lord Maximus. How are you enjoying the evening?" Both brothers had appeared to be handling their change in status quite well but looks could be deceiving.

"Very much, thank you. And you?"

"I had a lovely conversation with Miss St. Albans a short time ago. She mentioned that you and your brother embarked on the Grand Tour. What was your favorite city?"

"Rome."

"I've always wanted to see the Colosseum and the Forum, and...well, all of Rome." That was another dream that had been stored away.

"Roma è una città meravigliosa."

Oh dear. If she went weak in the knees at the sound of him speaking English, well this...she just might swoon.

The words escaped her lips with a breathy tone. *"Una città affascinante, dovrei pensare."*

Maximus stared at her in wonder. "You speak Italian?"

"Sì. Much to my mother's dismay and Warrington's delight, I studied everything I could. I don't believe there is a book in our library, or yours for that matter, that I have not read." It was how she passed the many lonely hours after her disastrous first season.

"Grandfather St. Albans had a passion for reading and a fondness for storytelling." Maximus gazed off into the distance as if recalling a memory. "When Lucius and I were young children, we would sit on Grandfather's lap while Larentia told us stories about legends and myths."

"Which is your favorite?" Sabina was enjoying the conversation, enjoying his company. She knew nothing of a romantic nature could ever happen, but she hoped they could at least be friends.

"The story of Romulus and Remus."

"Ah yes, the founders of Rome." That had been one of Sabina's favorites, too. It had sounded so romantic to a young girl's ears.

"You know the story?"

"Of course. Warrington has a passion for antiquities. When I was little, he would tell me all sorts of tales. I often wondered if he believed that, just like Romulus and Remus, you too would be returned home."

"I guess there are some similarities, except I don't have an evil uncle who tried to murder us, and I have no intention of disposing of my brother to secure the title."

"I suppose the legend is quite grim."

Maximus's velvety laughter rolled across her heart. "I suppose."

Soft chords from the orchestra drifted through the air, disrupting the moment. "It sounds as if the music is about to begin. I should—"

"Then may I have this dance, Miss Teverton?" Maximus bowed and extended his hand.

"I am a spinster, Lord Maximus. Men do not ask me to dance."

First Larentia, now Miss Teverton. What was it with women who declared themselves spinsters and refused to dance?

"I am a man and I have asked you to dance. Does that make me some sort of mythical creature? A griffon perhaps, or would you prefer something more exotic, such as a uni-wolf?"

Laughter escaped her lips, disrupting couples nearby, but Maximus didn't care. Miss Teverton was smiling. He'd make up eccentric mythical creatures every day to see the laughter and happiness in her eyes, the bright smile across her lips, and the adorable dimples kissing her cheeks.

"A uni-wolf?" she giggled.

"Yes, part unicorn, part wolf. It's a rare, intelligent, yet compassionate creature."

"I think you're a rare creature." The words escaped her lips a mere whisper and something electric charged between them. She blinked several times as she cleared her throat, her calm composure in place. "I believe one of the Darnell sisters would suit better." As she started to turn, he reached for her hand, attracting too much attention from those standing near, but he didn't care. He was not going to let Miss Teverton walk away from him. The *ton* would most likely attribute his lack of decorum to growing up in the country. Let the gossips think what they want, it would not keep him from dancing with her.

He gently kept hold of her gloved hand. "I don't want to dance with them. I want to dance with you."

She stared into his eyes. Her mouth formed a delicate "o" as she simply nodded her acquiescence.

The room hushed to a gentle hum as the music grew louder. It might be Maximus's imagination, but it seemed as if all eyes were centered on them. They completed the steps without faltering, circling this way, sashaying that way, and though no words were spoken, their bodies, their souls, spoke volumes to one another. Miss Teverton was indeed a rare creature— compassionate, well-read, could speak Italian, was enticingly beautiful, and unlike anyone he'd ever met. And he was desperate to know more.

As the dance came to an end, Maximus noticed Lucius strolling toward them, with Lady Graut following close behind.

"Good evening, Miss Teverton," Lucius said as he bowed slightly before turning to Maximus. "Lady Graut wanted to see us side by side," he whispered before the lady in question joined them.

Miss Teverton stiffened at the mention of Lady Graut's name. "Thank you for the dance, Lord Maximus. Enjoy the rest of your evening, Lord Lucius." And with that, she left their side, disappearing into the crush.

This is what his life had become—social obligations, endless gossip, and constantly being put on display. Lady Graut had even managed to scare off the one woman Maximus wanted to be near.

"It was quite exciting to hear that you both had been discovered," Lady Graut said as she waddled up to the pair. "And to think that, all this time, you were in England. His Grace is indeed a lucky man. Just think, two heirs, plus your uncle. I guess all that needs to be decided is which one of you is the oldest."

"I don't believe that mystery shall ever be solved since we were taken from our parents as infants. It's not as if there was a note attached declaring which was which." Maximus was tired of this conversation and based on the exaggerated yawn his brother had just executed, Lucius was as well.

"This has been a stimulating conversation, but we must greet the other guests in attendance." Lucius's tone bordered on rude.

Lady Graut waved her fan to stop their retreat and with another annoying giggle asked, "Before you take your leave, pray tell, which of you is Lord Maximus, and which is Lord Lucius?"

Maximus looked at his brother. It was a thoroughly enjoyable game they used to play as children which had not lost its luster through the years. "Why, I am Lucius," Maximus said with a wave of his hand and an elaborate bow, emulating his brother.

"Oh, I just knew it," Lady Graut said with another high-pitched giggle. "I can clearly see the difference between the two of you."

"Oh, you can?" Lucius questioned with a hint of sarcasm.

"Oh yes, Lord Maximus." Lady Graut continued on to delineate the subtle differences between Maximus and his brother, none of which were correct. By the time they were able to peel themselves away from her, they both were exhausted.

"Are we so similar that no one sees the difference between us?"

"I believe most only see the physical similarities, rather than the internal differences." One day, Maximus hoped to find a woman who saw him for him and not as a twin, identical in appearance to Lucius.

"Enough of this tedious conversation. It's time we enjoyed our new station." No sooner had Maximus raised a warning brow, Lucius replied, "Yes, I know. Don't do anything to disgrace our family." The lecture was truer now than ever.

When growing up, Maximus had always been aware of their position. They had been brought into a home and brought up by people who were not their family. They had been given an exceptional life, and Maximus believed it was their duty to be respectful and never cause Larentia or their adoptive grandfather grief. Sadly, his brother had not always shared those sentiments.

He watched as couples began assembling for the quadrille. As the music began, one pair caught his attention. He blinked several times. "I can't believe...I never would have..."

"Stop rambling," Lucius began as he followed Maximus's gaze. "Is that Larentia?"

"Yes."

"And she is dancing with Picus?" Lucius's tone of disbelief mirrored his own thoughts.

"Yes."

"I thought she claimed spinsters don't dance."

"I suppose she made an exception." Maximus was glad. Larentia had been through so much as of late, he wanted her to enjoy herself.

"Speaking of spinsters, I saw you conversing with Miss Teverton."

It was not a question, more of an observation, and Maximus knew exactly what his brother was up to. Lucius wanted information and would not just come out and ask about what was on his mind. Well, two could play at that game.

In turn, he questioned, "I saw you hanging onto every word Miss Cornelia was saying. She is attractive," he paused for a moment to annoy his brother before adding, "by *ton* standards."

"And what is that supposed to mean? You don't find Miss Cornelia beautiful? I'm told she's quite accomplished on the pianoforte..." Lucius's words died off as Maximus's laughter reverberated from his chest. "And what is so amusing, my dear brother?"

"Nothing, *my* dear brother. Only that I know what games you play. Be honest, Miss Cornelia is nothing more than an attractive lady with a handsome dowry, plenty of good manners, and the ability to only speak of the weather and state of the roads."

"I suppose you are correct in your observation." Lucius let out a long huff. "No, you're absolutely correct." He shook his head. "She went on and on for fifteen minutes about the weather in Bath and how it changes from season to season. If it weren't for her ample bosom, which was very nicely on display, I might have passed out from boredom."

"Perhaps there is more substance to you than I originally suspected."

"I certainly hope so, otherwise I might be doomed to a life with someone who only cares for title and good looks." He puffed out his chest with his self-endorsement.

"It is clear that whoever you marry must have an excellent sense of humor in order to deal with your inflated ego."

"I shall take that as a compliment and take my leave in search of beauty *and* intelligence. Good evening, dear brother."

Maximus was not going to tell his twin he had already discovered both in Miss Teverton.

Chapter Six

THE SMALL GATHERING with one of Lady March's dearest friends had turned into a rather large dinner party of sixty guests. Once word spread that the brothers were to attend the evening, the number of acceptances grew exponentially. Maximus highly doubted he and Lucius were as interesting as everyone claimed.

The conversation was the same as at their welcoming ball—who had taken the boys all those years ago? It was a tiresome question that would never be answered. Why couldn't the *ton* just accept it and move on to other gossip which did not include him or his brother?

Unlike Lucius, who had welcomed their change in status with open arms, hoping to indulge in everything he believed the grandson of a duke was entitled to— including lavish dinners, beautiful willing ladies, and ample funds. Maximus was growing weary of the continuous social demands. He longed for the country, quiet gatherings, and intellectual conversations. He was counting the hours until they left for Warrington Hall. It was one thing to be introduced to society at a grand ball, but quite another to make the rounds night after night. If accepting invitation after invitation, enduring sycophants who lurked in every drawing room and pasting on false smiles was the order of the *ton*, then he wanted nothing to do with this lifestyle. He suspected his brother would be pleased if he bowed out and took his place as spare, but he'd promised Larentia he'd keep an open mind.

"It is a pity Lord Lucius was unable to join us this evening," Lady Shafton commented as they paired up for dinner. Thankfully, he had not been paired with Lady Yendall who had mistaken him for Lucius. Instead he was subjugated to Lady Shafton's theories on the best tonics for what ailed Lucius.

"I'm sure he will be making the social rounds again soon enough." Maximus didn't believe his brother was ill any more than he believed the sky could turn red with a snap of his fingers, but he was not going to let Lady Shafton know the truth. Part of him wished he'd been clever enough to come up with an excuse and bow out this evening, to enjoy the comfort of the Warrington library, but he was not the master of tall tales.

The couples strolled into the dining room with much pomp and fanfare. With great efficiency, dinner was served by numerous footmen and the evening progressed as any hostess would have hoped.

One conversation blended into another as Maximus fought boredom. Tonight's festivities were testing how open-minded he could be. He was not used to this lifestyle of constantly having to pretend to be interested in the conversation of those around him. Every so often he nodded at Lady Shafton's commentary, hopefully giving the impression he was listening. Before too long, the conversation turned for the worse.... marriage. All eyes turned toward him, waiting for his opinion one way or another.

It wasn't that he was opposed to marriage, quite the contrary. In fact, he wanted to marry and have a family of his own. He *was*, however, opposed to the constant parade of ladies only interested in looks, fortune, and title. What about intelligence, common interests, attraction?

One lady was eager to point out her list of the most suitable heiresses. "Yes, and do not forget Miss Darnell and Miss Volante. It is their first season, and both have substantial dowries."

His mother assertively entered the conversation at this point. "Neither of my sons are in need of a woman with a substantial dowry." Her words softened. "I would rather they marry for affection and love, than money."

The words reached Maximus's heart as his gaze settled on his mother. She offered a sincere smile. He did not doubt her words or the affection she still had for their father.

"Well, if money is not an issue, then there are other ladies who are more accomplished and would serve them greater," Lady Rodale stated, just before she took in a deep breath and presented *her* list of the most accomplished debutantes this season.

Once again, the conversation swirled about him as if he were not present. He didn't even try to engage or acknowledge the topic being discussed, but instead tried to distract his mind with thoughts of his grandfather's estate. Was His Grace one to sit back and let a land steward handle his affairs, or did he take an active part in the running of his estates? Would Maximus be able to implement some of the same improvements as he had at St. Albans, or would his ideas lay dusty and unfulfilled?

"Yes, and after that unfortunate incident with Lord Oxnard, the Cursed Heiress was permanently put on the shelf. Oh, don't mistake me, she's—"

"I do wish you would take greater care in how you speak of Miss Teverton."

The mention of Miss Teverton's name brought Maximus out of his reflection. What did Lady Rodale just say and why was mother so defensive?

Redness tainted Lady Rodale's features as she spoke, "I apologize, Lady March, I forgot how close the two of you are."

"Please do not forget that in the future." His mother's firm words silenced Lady Rodale.

An uncomfortable stillness enveloped the room for several minutes before Lord Rodale decided to rescue his wife from further embarrassment, changing the topic of conversation entirely. "I daresay Miss Bellingsworth is the finest soprano we've heard in quite some time. Wouldn't you agree?" He questioned to no one in particular.

With the tension in the room easing slightly, the dinner conversation resumed to include nonsensical topics, including who would be excluded from Lady Farland's ball, and who might be responsible for Miss C's abrupt departure from society.

The evening passed in slow torturous measures. By the time Maximus and his mother were ensconced in the ducal carriage, he thought his head would explode. However, there was *one* topic of conversation he was curious about.

"What was said about Miss Teverton that had you so upset?"

"Just some unfortunate, and might I add entirely false, rumors that circulated the *ton* during Miss Teverton's first season." His mother quickly changed the subject. "Tell me about your travels to the Continent. What did you enjoy most?"

Maximus would have rather heard more about Miss Teverton, but if he'd learned one thing about his mother thus far, it was that she was persistent in her quest to find out all she could about Maximus and Lucius. He would bide his time for now and indulge her. "The architecture, especially that of ancient Roman times. It is impressive to see the accomplishments and ingenuity of men who lived so long ago."

"Your father was quite fascinated with architecture as well. He had dreamed of building a structure of his own design, but his drawing skills with pen and paper were lacking at best." She let out a giggle. "My darling Martin tried to no end to improve."

"Do you still have his plans?" Maximus was desperate to know the father he would never be able to meet.

"Why yes, of course. Warrington and I saved all of Martin's things. They're at Warrington Hall. I'll show you his drawings if you'd care to see them?" Mother's excitement was contagious.

"That would be very agreeable."

"You're very much like him." The words filled the carriage as sadness lingered in his heart.

It wasn't the first time someone had said that to him. "Grandfather and Miss Teverton said something similar. How are we alike?"

There was a short pause before Mother spoke. "Well, you look like him, but that goes without saying. But it goes beyond that. Your manners and presence, but especially the way you seem to care for others, and give so much of yourself."

"Are you referring to Larentia?"

Her body stiffened. "Yes." He heard the sorrow in her voice, the heartache of a mother who had not been able to raise her sons. "I have no intention of replacing the special place she holds in your heart, but I do hope with time..."

Maximus took his mother's petite gloved hand in his. "You already have a special place and it's growing larger every day."

"That's something your father would have said." She sniffled as she spoke. "He always made those around him feel special."

"Well, you are."

Maximus was enjoying this intimate time with his mother, and hearing stories about his father. His insides still fought a silent battle between the life he'd been brought up with and the one he was slowly assimilating into. Perhaps Larentia was right and he just needed more time and to not think so much.

As they entered the ducal residence, Larentia's fallen features and worried eyes signaled there was trouble and Maximus knew exactly who was at the center of it.

"Where is he?"

"I don't know for certain, but I suspect—"

"Hell's." Maximus ran a frustrated hand through his hair. "Damn him," he swore as he turned away from his mother.

"Hell's?" his mother questioned. "Not as in Hell's Gaming House?" Her voice rose an octave with each word spoken. "That place is nothing but trouble." The worry in her tone pierced his heart.

"I'll handle this." He stormed from the house with only one destination in mind.

Between Lady Yendall who, believing he was Lucius, cornered him, and made sexual innuendos before offering her services as a mistress, and his brother sneaking out of the house to gamble at one of the most infamous gambling hells in London, it had not been a good night.

Hell's Gaming House was notorious for high-stake gambling, and pleasure seeking at whatever cost. Maximus was worried that Lucius would test how high the latter could go.

By the time he reached the establishment, his mood had soured further. He would pay off Lucius's losses, pour the idiot into the carriage, and then beat some sense into him. In that order.

He stormed into the gaudy foyer, pushing past curious onlookers. The air was thick with illicit activity as women and money vied for attention.

"Good evening, Lord Lucius, it is a pleasure to have you here this evening," one of the employees said as Maximus attempted to regain his composure and casually stroll into the main room to look for his brother.

He blinked several times, then turned to the man. "What did you just say? What name did you use?"

Fear streaked across the man's face. "Lord Lucius." He swallowed hard as dawning set in. "You're n...not Lord Lucius?" Beads of sweat formed on his brow. Maximus couldn't blame this man for the mistake, but he could call out his brother.

"Where is my brother?" he growled in a low tone. *So much for composure.*

He held a hand in front of him. "This way, Lord Maximus."

Maximus was guided into the main hall and in no time at all, he spotted Lucius, who was completely enthralled in his game at the Faro table. Crossing his arms, Maximus strolled up to his brother and waited.

Lucius must have sensed his presence, for he turned around very slowly and looked up at him. His face was emotionless, but his blue eyes were seeped with guilt.

"How dare you come here and use my name." Maximus wasn't a saint, but he always lived within proper boundaries.

"You don't need to get upset, we're winning." Lucius's lighthearted tone did not strike the right chord with Maximus.

"Get up, you're finished here."

Pushing his chair out, Lucius stood. Brandy and cheroot were mingled on his body and breath. "You are not my keeper." His words were slow, not quite slurred.

Maximus was in no mood to play this game with his brother...again. He swung his fist and with one swift punch Lucius swiveled to the ground. All activity around them halted as stares settled on them. There would be rumors about which brother hit the other, but Maximus didn't care. Let them stare. Let them gossip. Perhaps then his brother would learn.

He pulled his unconscious twin off the floor, hoisted him over his shoulder, and stormed out. He was furious. No, furious was too mild a word.

He tossed Lucius into the elegant ducal carriage, then growled to the driver, "Let's go."

"Ow!" A moan escaped Lucius's lips as he struggled onto the seat.

"Jaw hurts?"

"Bastard," Lucius spat out.

Maximus had to resist the urge to knock his twin out again. He flexed his knuckles, then quickly tucked them away. He might still punch Lucius, but first he needed answers.

"What the hell do you think you were doing back there?"

"Playing Faro."

"And using my name? What did you hope to accomplish?"

"Since I already made Grandfather angry once, I needed some assurance in case I lost again."

The words rumbled from Maximus's mouth, "By claiming you were ill, sneaking out of the house, and ruining my good name at Hell's."

"Yes, your good name. It is always about *your* good name."

"When we return, you will apologize to Larentia, and then you *will* speak to Grandfather and explain what you've done."

"You're not in charge of me," Lucius said with a slight pout.

"Then start acting your age and make responsible..." Maximus did not finish his lecture as the carriage came to an abrupt halt. The door flew open revealing their grandfather.

There was no word to describe the state the older man was in.

"What in bloody hell did you think you were doing?" The anger ricocheted off the small interior space. "In my study. Now."

Grandfather turned and within moments disappeared inside expecting the brothers to follow without resistance. Maximus did not have to look behind to know Lucius was following, sulking and with his tail between his legs.

In hindsight, Maximus should have controlled his rage and not punched his brother in Hell's. But that which could not be undone was his mistake. As he entered the study, he sucked in a breath, preparing for the onslaught of his grandfather's full wrath.

He didn't have to wait long.

"I did not wait twenty-three years for this!" The Duke turned his full attention on Lucius, whose eye was showing signs of a bruise. For one brief moment Maximus felt sorry for his brother. "How dare you think so little of me, of your mother, and Miss St. Albans that you feel the need to lie and act like a sneak."

Maximus was not about to tell Grandfather how Lucius had used his name at Hell's. The Duke would probably hear the gossip soon enough. He would not make things worse for his brother. That minor detail was between him and Lucius, and he would deal with that later.

Lucius kept his head hung low, his features stricken. "I apologize, Grandfather. It will not happen again."

"No, it won't." Grandfather inhaled deeply, as if trying to control his anger. "We're setting off for the country, where I hope your behavior will improve." He then turned to Maximus, his tone softened and not holding any of the fury that had just been unleashed on Lucius. "And in the future, you will let Picus handle these indiscretions."

"Yes, Grandfather." His pride had been bruised by not only Lucius's behavior, but his own.

"Maximus, you may leave. I wish to have a talk with Lucius."

By the next morning, Maximus's mood had not improved. He was at a loss as to what he should do about Lucius, who would not confide in him about what happened after he'd left their grandfather's study. He felt responsible for his brother. Always had. Whenever Lucius had been punished for some trouble he'd stirred, Maximus had felt his pain. How was he going to get it through Lucius's thick skull that being the grandson of a duke did not entitle him to be careless?

He hoped a brisk morning walk under a clear blue sky would improve his spirits and prepare him for the coming tedious day of yet more introductions, lessons on the Warrington heritage, and proper *ton* etiquette.

An hour later, his body was relaxed and his thoughts a little clearer. Once they were in the country, Lucius would not have access to such vices as Hell's and the abundance of ladies vying for his attention. They would spend their days exploring the home their father grew up in, going for rides, and spending time together. Things would improve. Maximus only hoped his brother could control himself until then.

He'd just rounded the corner, nearing the ducal residence, when he spied an intriguing figure in a green walking dress casually strolling away from him. *Miss Teverton.* Although they were residing under the same roof, he had not had much opportunity to speak with her, to spend time with her.

"Good morning, Miss Teverton," he called to her breaking one of the lessons he'd endured on proper salutations.

She turned around, her enticing eyes meeting his, and for a brief moment, all sounds around them halted. He wondered if she felt the same.

"Good morning, Lord Maximus. You're out rather early this morning."

Maximus strolled to her, drawn in by her bright smile and sensuous dimples. "I enjoy walking first thing while much of the *ton* is still fast asleep." He brushed off the fact that she'd probably guessed which twin she was addressing. After all, she had a fifty-fifty chance. "I thought ladies were supposed to have a chaperone?"

"Only eligible ones. I'm firmly on the shelf, so there are certain benefits."

"How can you be on the shelf?" The woman standing beside him was intelligent and beautiful, well-spoken and sincere, and she clearly believed that she *was* a spinster.

"By the time a woman reaches my age—"

"You talk as if you have one foot in the grave. Could I tempt you to reveal your years?"

A slight chuckle escaped her lips. "Didn't Miss St. Albans teach you it is impolite to ask a person's age?"

"I must have been ill that day," he responded with a gentle tease, hoping Miss Teverton would relax with him.

"I suppose I *could* humor you." She lowered her voice and looked around for....well, he didn't know for what, but he was enjoying this playful side to her. "I'm thirty."

"I dare say you look remarkably well for someone of your advanced years. Better than well, in fact." She was like a painting in the Uffizi, absolute perfection.

Amusement flickered in her eyes as she tilted her head to one side and smiled, revealing the dimples he adored so much. "Why thank you, Lord Maximus."

"May I escort you home?" He didn't really want to return. He'd rather spend the day getting to know Miss Teverton, but duty called.

She nodded her head.

His mind could not comprehend why someone with Miss Teverton attributes had never married. The question lingered on the tip of his tongue. It wasn't like him to blurt things out. "Why haven't you married?" But blurt he did.

Her hand went to her lips, but rather than angry words, laughter escaped her lips. "I believe your lack of manners may get you in trouble one day."

"I hope so," he added with the half-smile that had never failed him in the past.

"It is rather fortunate for you that I do not mind sharing what some may consider delicate details." She swayed away from him, shifting her balance from one foot to another. Her movements were graceful and enticing in all the same step, and then she revealed, "I suppose you haven't heard." She paused, looking directly at him. "I'm cursed."

"Cursed?" He had heard. Lady Rodale had sufficiently refreshed everyone's memory last night. He'd been curious, but his mother had remained tight-lipped when he questioned her.

"Yes, quite cursed I'm afraid." Her tone was almost playful. Maximus was confused by the mixture of thoughts and emotions coursing through his mind and body.

"And why are you considered cursed?"

"Because of these," she said as she pointed to her eyes.

"You don't believe that, do you?" Maximus thought her eyes most extraordinary, not in the least the sign of a curse.

She stopped, and once again turned her gaze on him. "It doesn't matter what I believe. The *ton* believes it."

"What happened to earn such disdain from those old biddies who supposedly rule the finer class?"

"I would not let them hear you say that," she said with a giggle before continuing, "you may find yourself at the top of the scandal sheets." Her tone turned serious. On a long exhale, she began, "I was engaged to Lord Oxnard—"

"You were engaged?" Maximus did not like the thought of Miss Teverton being with another man, kissed by another man, held... *Where had that thought come from?*

"Only briefly."

"What does that have to do with being cursed?"

"When the man you're engaged to supposedly has a fall from a horse and ends up with a broken arm and leg, the first thing he does is place blame rather than accept responsibility for his less than appropriate actions."

"*Supposedly* fell from his horse?" He could hear the incredulous tone in his own voice.

"It is rumored he was with his mistress. They had an argument about his inebriated state and fell down the stairs. He never quite recovered, still walks with a limp."

"And what do you believe?"

Miss Teverton began to step away, slowly increasing the distance between them, as she replied matter-of-factly, "Since he was discovered on the foyer floor, I find it hard to believe that his horse was the culprit. To counteract his father's fury, Lord Oxnard said I was the cause of all his woes, that the Cursed Heiress had struck again."

"Surely the *ton* did not believe such a ludicrous story?"

"Of course, they did, and my own mother aided their opinions." The sadness in her voice lingered in his heart.

"Why would she do such a thing?"

"Since the day I was born, she has always believed I brought ill-fortune to her." Miss Teverton spoke softly then shifted her gaze to the ground, attempting to avoid further discussion.

He'd been wanting to discover what, or rather who, had caused her grief when they first met. He suspected he knew the answer. "Is that who upset you at the theatre?"

She nodded.

"Why does your mother believe you're cursed?"

"Her own mother died rather suddenly the day I was born." She continued to keep her gaze turned away from him.

"But that's just a coincidence," he began to argue in Miss Teverton's defense, but she shook her head.

"That was not the only incident. There were many through the years. The earliest one I remember was when I accidently walked in on my mother with her lover."

"How old were you?"

"Five. I didn't understand what I saw, so I went crying to my father." Her words were full of such sorrow. She raised her eyes and met his gaze. "Anytime anything bad happened, Mother just knew I had something to do with it."

Maximus reached out, desperately wanting to comfort her. He placed his hand on her shoulder for the briefest of moments before quickly forcing it to his side. The street may be quite deserted this time of morning, but it did not mean that gossips were not lurking.

"It doesn't take long for the *ton* to follow suit, and the invitations to stop. I got tired of all the stares, the gossip, the cruel innuendos, so I retreated from society and put my dream of finding love on the shelf."

It seemed like such a lonely existence to Maximus to never have passion or intimacy. "But you're missing out on so much."

Miss Teverton stepped away from him, continuing to try and widen the gap between them. "Only if you don't know what you're missing."

He closed the distance, desperate to not let her retreat, and looked directly at her, holding her attention, stoking a gently growing fire. "I believe you're wrong." And he was going to prove it to her.

Chapter Seven

SABINA HAD TOILED with this dilemma the entire day, but now that her mind was made up, she was dreading informing her dearest friend of her decision. Every time Maximus was near, her heart was at risk. He saw past her eyes and straight to her soul. He talked *to* her, not at her. And when she told him about the curse he dismissed the affliction, giving no weight to it or the gossips who continually resurrected a lifetime of heartache. Sabina feared she was already half in love with him.

Since the old hunting cottage would soon be ready, it seemed a natural decision to move into it early given all the changes in the Warrington household.

Sucking in her breath, she trudged up to the door and knocked softly.

The door opened wide a moment later, revealing a rather unkept room and disheveled Sylvia—both of which were quite out of the ordinary. "Oh, I'm relieved you're here. There is still so much to organize before our departure in the morning. I don't want to forget anything." She rushed about her private parlor, moving this item, packing that item, but nothing seemed to be getting done.

Better to get this conversation over with before the knot in Sabina's stomach swelled and consumed her entire body. "I...um, I don't want to trouble you, but..." *Oh, just tell her.* "I...I was thinking..." Her words drifted as Sylvia turned around, the joyous expression that had appeared since she learned her sons were alive instantly turning to unease.

"What's the matter?" Sylvia smoothed back her hair with her hand.

Sabina worried the edge of her sleeve. "I've been pondering this for the past couple of weeks." She inhaled deeply, then let the words tumble from her mouth. "I believe it best I reside at Teverton cottage once we're back in the country. You will be—"

"No." The single word was quick, firm, and bespoke no argument.

"No?" Her voice rose in surprise.

Sylvia let out a little sigh as she approached Sabina, her features eased, her words caring. "I don't want you to feel like you are no longer welcome now that my sons have returned."

"But you will be preoccupied with getting to know them, organizing the house party, all the guests, and—"

"And that's precisely why I need you." She took Sabina's hands in hers. "I need you to help me through this. No one understands better than you what the past twenty-three years have been like for me. For both of us. We need each other. That has not changed."

Better to accept reality now, than an uncomfortable situation later when told she was no longer welcome at Warrington. She let out a long sigh. "I can't reside with you forever. At some—"

"You will always be welcome in our homes." Sylvia's tone softened. "You are my family, too. I can not imagine you not being part of my life, not seeing you every day."

Sylvia's words tugged at her heart strings. She should decline and accept what Fate had offered. Long, silent seconds passed as she contemplated what she *should* do versus what she *wanted* to do. In the end, she gave into her heart.

Sabina didn't know if she was making the correct choice, but it was nice to be needed, to be loved. "Then I will stay." She was not one for flowery speeches or expressing her sentiments. She'd learned a long time ago that only led to heartache, but this was different. She knew her dearest friend was sincere. They'd been through quite a lot together. "Thank you for saying I'm part of your family. It means a great deal to me."

"I know, dearest. I hope one day you will find happiness and have a family of your own, but until then, you will always be welcome in mine."

A family of her own. For as long as she could remember, she'd always loved being around babies and children. Their sweet innocence and candid explanations made the world a better, happier, less cruel place.

"I believe that book has closed and —"

Sylvia squeezed her hand as she shook her head. "Perhaps a chapter, but not the book. Trust me on this. What happened all those years ago was not your fault. You could not have stopped those events, you were just a child." Sylvia hugged her. "And despite what you think, you still have plenty of time to find love."

Sabina nodded her head to appease Sylvia, but she had accepted the truth. The guilt from twenty-three years ago was still too palpable, and she definitely did not believe love was in her future. It was always better to be realistic.

A firm knock sounded on the door, followed by the appearance of Picus. "Your sons wish to have a moment of your time, Lady March."

Sylvia had never been one to hide her emotions, and the mention of her sons was no exception. Every time their names were spoken, her face lit up, and features softened. Sabina was happy her dearest friend had been reunited with her children after all these years, but she felt as if she was losing her at the same time.

Sabina sucked in her breath, determined to keep her thoughts to herself, and politely began to excuse herself. "I'll take my leave—"

Sylvia reached for her hand again, holding it firmly within her own as if to make a point. "I meant what I said, I would be heartbroken if you decided to leave."

Bright sunlight and gentle rolling hills welcomed them as they passed through the quiet countryside en route to Warrington Hall. Maximus was amazed by the splendor of nature, the abundance of trees and wildlife, and the heady scent of earth mingled with the crisp country air. He'd never been to this part of the country before. His legs itched to go and explore, but most of all, he was thankful for the time alone with his brother and Larentia before their lives would once again be turned upside down.

Thankfully Grandfather and Mother had travelled ahead to Warrington Hall in order to make arrangements for their arrival and plan an elaborate house party to welcome Maximus and his brother back into the bosom of their family. Aunts, uncles, cousins, and friends would all be descending in the coming days. Unfortunately, Sabina had also adjourned with them. The only consolation was he would have more time with her in the country. One moment she was happy and talkative, in the next, her mood would darken, and she became distant. And when he tried to garner information from his mother, grandfather, or even Picus in regard to Sabina, they too quickly changed the topic.

"Nothing will be the same." Larentia's ominous words came over the sound of carriage wheels rolling rapidly.

"Do you regret leaving London so soon?"

"No." She looked at Maximus. "Truth be told, I was dreading living in Town. It's too hectic and crowded. I much prefer the peace of the countryside."

Maximus heard the remorse in her voice and hoped he mistook the meaning. "You're not blaming yourself for not taking us to Town sooner?"

She glanced away, feigning interest in the passing countryside. Several seconds passed before she replied, "No...yes." Her brown eyes met his. "If I had tried to convince my father that London was a vital part of your education, someone might have recognized you sooner, and then you would have been reunited with your mother, with your family, all that much sooner."

"But then we would have missed the opportunity to have you and Grandfather in our life. I wouldn't have changed a thing."

"I wouldn't change a thing either," Lucius jumped into the conversation. "Except perhaps the chance to mingle with the fairer sex more often."

"There is a reason I didn't want you let loose, Lucius. You would have no doubt been quite the rake about town. Who knows what trouble you would have found."

"Perhaps you're right, Larentia." Lucius's tone turned remorseful as he glanced Maximus's way. "It *is* probably for the best that we're leaving. And besides, what could possibly happen in the boring countryside?"

Although things were still strained between him and Lucius over everything that happened at Hell's, at least his brother was talking to him again and putting on a good front for everyone else.

"I am curious about something," Maximus said, garnering attention from Lucius and Larentia. "What made you change your mind about dancing?"

For the first time he could recall, Larentia blushed, and not just a subtle pinking of the cheeks, but a fierce flare that encompassed her features. She worried at her gloved fingers. "It was nice to receive attention from a handsome gentleman."

Lucius being Lucius, took the opportunity to tease. "If I didn't know better, I'd say you have a schoolgirl crush on Picus."

"I would have to agree with you, dear brother," Maximus chimed in, enjoying the playful banter.

"Oh, you two are quite the scoundrels." Laughter filled the carriage. It was a nice change to be removed from the city and for a brief time forget that he and Lucius were heirs to the Duke of Warrington.

Pleasant hours passed as they journeyed toward their destination. In the distance, an impressive structure stood. Although they were still quite some distance away, Maximus could sense the splendor and magnificence of the structure. Warrington Hall stood proud on the hill, almost too proud and slightly ostentatious.

"The house has a fascinating history." Larentia went on to explain that in the first half of the eighteenth century, the fourth Duke of Warrington had commissioned the home to be built in the same style of Nonsuch Palace at a cost of nearly twenty thousand pounds.

"What was so important about Nonsuch Palace that the fourth duke would expend such a vast amount of money?" Lucius said with awe as he gazed out the carriage window.

"Nonsuch Palace was built by Henry VIII. It was said that none could match its extravagance and perfection. I suppose the fourth duke believed his residence could."

Maximus listened as Larentia weaved the tale of how Nonsuch Palace came to be, imagining how it compared to Warrington Hall. As they neared their ancestral home, more architectural details came into focus. The eight-sided towers at each end of the south façade rose to touch the sky while the vast lawn spread out before them, welcoming them home. He was enthralled with the structure, and hoped the plans had been preserved.

Almost a half hour passed before the carriage came to a halt in front of the magnificent structure. Efficient servants prepared the steps, and before Maximus could even step foot on the ground, Grandfather, with their mother by his side, emerged from the entry, all smiles and well-wishes.

"You must be tired from your journey," Mother said as she approached them. "After you've been introduced to the staff, you will be able to have a short rest. Some of the guests have already begun to arrive, but you will have a couple of days to get acquainted with your surroundings before the house party officially begins." The excitement in her voice was palpable. It was clear she'd been waiting a long time to have her children part of her life once again.

"Thank you," they all said in unison, each uncertain what to say next.

A rather tall man with wavy grey hair and deep brown—almost black—eyes emerged from the house just behind their grandfather. He looked to be in his mid-fifties. His features were similar to Grandfather's, yet distinctively different. Must be one of the numerous relatives they were to be introduced to at the house party.

Mother turned. "This is Lord Daniel, your father's brother."

An uncle.

"I cannot begin to express how relieved I am you've been found after all these years. I apologize for not being able to join you in London, but estate business in the north kept me away." Although Lord Daniel's words and tone of voice sounded sincere, there was something about him that Maximus instantly didn't like. It wasn't anything in particular, but just a feeling he couldn't quite define.

Lucius shot Maximus a stony glare before he masked his features and greeted their father's brother with over enthusiasm. "It's grand to finally meet you, Uncle Daniel."

His twin's actions only served to further aggravate him. Once again, Lucius embraced this relative without concern. Surely Lucius must sense what he did—their thoughts had never strayed this far apart.

Then again, perhaps he was just tired from the journey. He shook off the feeling. He'd only just met his uncle and had no reason to think ill of him. A short rest followed by a long walk should help with whatever was ailing him, it always had in the past. And perhaps, if he were fortunate enough, he would encounter Miss Teverton.

The afternoon sunlight soaked into Sabina's soul, warming her, easing her worries. The cool breeze rustled through the leaves, the soft sounds of nature a balm. At this moment, she felt peace. She had missed the country.

As she wandered on a secluded path toward the hedge maze, she reflected on everything that happened and the many changes that were sure to come. She had also come to an important decision since arriving in the country. Sabina would continue to reside with Sylvia but would not return to London...ever.

On those occasions when the family traveled to Town, she would take her leave and retire at the cottage. Sabina would slowly remove herself from their lives altogether. It was for the best, she reminded herself yet again. One day Lord Maximus would marry and, although she would be happy for him, she did not believe she was strong enough to endure that heartache.

The path weaved through a small grouping of trees before sloping to the maze. It was one of her favorite spots, second only to the temple the previous Duke of

Warrington had built, but that was an adventure for another day.

She had just rounded the corner, about to enter the maze, when a deep familiar voice greeted her. "Good afternoon, Miss Teverton."

Sabina's body warmed further at the sound of Maximus's voice. Her breath caught in her throat as she turned around. He cut such a handsome figure in a navy-blue coat, which made his eyes seem even bluer, if that were possible. "Good afternoon, Lord Maximus. When did you arrive?" The space between his brows crinkled. Could she have offended him with her question? She quickly added a pleasantry, hoping to ease the look of bewilderment. "It is a pleasant day to be out enjoying nature, is it not?"

"We arrived just a short time ago. It was too fine an afternoon to stay inside. But I'm curious about something." He seemed to waiver for a moment, as if what he was curious about was entirely inappropriate. Truth be told, Sabina would like to experience something entirely inappropriate with him. *Oh dear,* she really should learn to control her thoughts.

"Yes?"

Lord Maximus strolled up to her. "How did you know I'm Maximus? It's the third time you've addressed me as...well, me. We've only recently met and no one, except Larentia, has ever been able to tell the difference between my brother and I." His eyes gleamed with admiration.

Warmth rushed her cheeks as her heartbeat quickened. *Stop being foolish.* Lord Maximus would never be interested in a spinster with mismatched eyes. *Remember your plan.*

She swallowed hard, begging her pulse to steady. "Your voice. It's different to your brothers." He raised a quizzical brow, and she added, "It's a little deeper, only slightly, but I noticed it the first time we met. Plus, you seem to favor wearing dark blue. I take note of these things."

"What sort of things?"

"People's voices mostly."

"Why?"

"It was never an issue prior, but after you and your brother were stolen, I could hardly sleep, too afraid I'd be next. I would listen carefully to the sounds of night, memorizing voices. I..." The rapid pounding in her chest reminded her this conversation was turning too personal. She needed to quickly change the subject before she revealed too much. "What's it like being a twin?"

"It was quite fun when we were younger, being able to confuse people and pretend to be each other, but as we got older, we just wanted to be unique."

"I can understand that." Her confession earned her his surprise.

"You can?"

"Of course, I would think that so many people would want to be known as individuals." Sabina stopped for a moment and thought about the words that just left her mouth, and then retracted. "Actually, no."

"Pardon?"

She pulled a leaf from an obliging bush and worried it between her fingers. "I don't believe most want to be seen as unique and individual. I believe people want to be associated with what's popular rather than discovering who they are."

"Not you." It wasn't a question, but a statement.

"No. I want to be exactly who I am." *And to be accepted for who I am.* But that too was a dream for another life.

"That is admirable." The warmth in his voice heated her insides. It would be far too easy to succumb to his compliments, to give into her heart's desire.

"Clearly, you're not speaking of me," Lord Lucius said as he strolled up to them.

"I don't believe admirable is synonymous with Lucius," Lord Maximus teased, earning a chuckle from his brother. Soft laughter bubbled from within Sabina.

"Miss Teverton had just been sharing a trait she developed after the kidnapping." Two sets of identical blue eyes settled on her with Lord Maximus's comment.

"Do you remember when we were taken?" There was a rushed anxiousness to Lord Lucius's tone that she simply could not ignore.

She supposed it was natural for him, for both of them, to want to know what had happened that night, but there were some things she just would not reveal. She would say just enough to pacify their curiosity and nothing more. Anything more could ignite the nightmares.

"Yes." The coldness she'd felt that night crept back into her soul. After the twins had been taken, she had not slept without a candle lit for more than a year, crying herself to sleep for fear she might be taken too. Her thoughts drifted back to that night. She'd been so excited to see the babies, she'd talked her father's ear off during the carriage ride there.

"How old were you?" Lord Lucius's question brought her back to the present.

"Seven." She could still hear Sylvia's cries in her sleep, and her own mother's hurtful words, words she would never tell another living soul. Words that would stay buried in her soul.

"What happened?" Maximus's tone softened. "Please."

Remembrances of the nanny's lifeless body slumped on the chair...heart-wrenching screams echoing through the furthest recesses of her mind. "I don't know anything else. I'm sorry."

The quivering started deep in her stomach and grew exponentially as panic enveloped her entire being. She couldn't speak, could barely breath as the nightmare tried to force its way to the surface.

Without thought for propriety, she turned and fled. She'd thought she could keep her emotions under control. Clearly, she was wrong.

She heard them call out to her, but she ran further into the maze, twisting through the labyrinth until she found solitude. The temple at the center of the maze had always been her sanctuary. No one ventured there, so she knew she was safe. Safe to let her emotions consume her without the embarrassment of appearing weak.

Chapter Eight

DINNER HAD PASSED without incident, despite some tension ricocheting between Lucius and Maximus. Sabina did not know what had transpired, but Lady Beatrice felt the need to enlighten the ladies after the men adjourned for brandy.

"From what I understand, one is not pleased the other has embraced a certain relative who has a propensity for stirring unpleasantness."

Before any of the ladies present could tempt further information from Lady Beatrice, Sylvia walked into the room, putting to rest the said entertainment. Whether she heard or not, Sylvia gave no indication. With a gracious smile, she said, "The gentleman will be joining us momentarily, and Miss Colyer has agreed to entertain us on the pianoforte."

Sabina took a seat in a quiet corner toward the back of the room and waited for the music to begin. It was just easier this way. She'd learned to accept her lot as a spinster years ago. It seemed the more she had tried to be accepted, to take part, the more she was ostracized.

As the men began to trickle in and rejoin the ladies, she noticed Lord Herbert scuttle toward his wife. "You'll never believe what I just heard," the words rushed from his mouth with high-pitched excitement.

Lady Herbert practically jumped out of her seat. "Oh, do tell!"

Sabina had learned to avoid this particular gossipmonger during her first season. Unfortunately, they lived in this part of the county and Sylvia always felt obligated to invite them to the annual house party.

And holding true to form, Lord and Lady Herbert always accepted the invitation.

"Lord Oxnard has finally found love and is due to marry two weeks hence."

"That is wonderful news," Lady Herbert exclaimed. "After that unfortunate accident that left him practically a cripple, I had my doubts. Hopefully this engagement will have a better outcome than the last."

Had everyone forgotten that Lord Oxnard was with his mistress then? That Sabina had nothing to do with it? Would she never have peace? Tears stung her eyes. She would not stay and endure such torture.

Blinking several times to stamp down the tears, she casually made her way out of the room. The moment she entered the hall, she breathed a sigh of relief, thankful she escaped without notice.

"Anything the matter, my dear." She turned around at the sound of Warrington's caring voice, hoping he would not notice her discomposure. She didn't even manage to say one word before he offered his arm. "Let's go for a stroll."

Sabina accepted his arm, the warmth a comfort as it had always been. The Duke had become like the father she'd lost. Fearing her resolve would break, she swallowed hard and bit back the tears. It certainly wouldn't be the first time.

When they neared the tapestry gallery, clear of prying eyes, Warrington questioned, "What happened to upset you?"

"Why won't the past rest? I didn't do anything wrong, and yet I continue to pay for an indiscretion I didn't commit."

"I wish I could answer that, but all I can do is offer friendship and love." He brought her within his embrace.

"I'm sorry for being so foolish," she whispered against his chest, the steady beat of his heart a calming lullaby.

"You're not foolish, you're human." Warrington tightened his embrace. "Sylvia told me your concerns about the return of my grandsons. You have nothing to fear, you will always be welcome here."

Sabina lifted her head and looked into Warrington's caring blue eyes. "Why have you always been so kind to me?"

"You're like a granddaughter to me. After everything that happened, it was you who brought life to our existence. Sylvia and I..." He choked on his words. "Well...we would have been quite lost without you, my dear."

Sabina wrapped her arms around Warrington. It was nice to know she was loved.

"I'll make excuses if anyone asks after you." He kissed the top of her head, before disappearing down the hall, returning to his guests.

When Maximus rejoined the ladies, he was hoping for a moment to apologize to Sabina for upsetting her earlier in the day when she had run from him and Lucius, disappearing into the maze. It had taken them almost an hour to find their way out. Upon their return to the house, Maximus sought Picus and inquired after the design concept for the maze. He would be prepared the next time Sabina ran away.

Before dinner, Sabina had kept her distance, clinging to Lady Ealda, an elderly widow who monopolized her with tales of bygone days. Maximus had hoped to be partnered with her for dinner, but they were seated at opposite ends of the table. And now, she was no place to be seen.

Maximus strolled toward his mother when Lord and Lady Herbert's chattering about the upcoming nuptials of Lord Oxnard reached his ears. His stomach sank. Could that be why Sabina was not in the room?

With the guests distracted preparing for the entertainment, Maximus decided to search for Sabina.

Instinct told him to go in the opposite direction of all the talking, down the quiet, dimly lit hall. He'd just reached the tapestry gallery when he spotted Sabina in the arms of...his grandfather. His blood began to boil. He was old enough to be...well, *her* grandfather.

Common sense begged to be heard. There had to be an explanation, and he would get it tonight.

He ducked into an obliging room as the pair parted ways. He waited a couple of minutes before searching her out. He knew she had not returned the way he'd just come, so he decided to investigate, starting at the opposite end of the tapestry gallery.

Strolling down the gallery, a cool breeze brushed against his cheek halting his progress. A faint glimmer of moonlight streaked across the floor, providing a path to the open balcony door. His heart quickened at the sight of the silhouette of a female leaning against the balustrade.

Sabina.

"I didn't expect to find you out here." He attempted a casual tone as he strolled onto the balcony.

She whipped around, her hand stretched across her heaving chest. "Oh, I didn't hear anyone." A halfhearted smile crossed her lips. "I...it was rather stuffy."

"Yes, the number of guests is quite large. I can't imagine what it will be like when everyone is in attendance."

"I was referring to the conversation." Her tone was laced with hurt. So, she had heard the comments. Could what he'd just witnessed be as simple as Grandfather comforting her?

"I saw you with my grandfather." The words rushed from his mouth in an accusatory tone. "Why was he comforting you?"

Anger flashed in her eyes. "Are you spying on me?"

"No." He should really learn to measure his words *before* he spoke.

"Then what? Clearly you don't trust me."

He grabbed her arm before she could turn from him. "You know that's not true." He hoped she did not detect the guilt that laced his words. "I was concerned." She glanced down at his hand upon her arm with a harsh stare. He quickly released his grip. Damn, he was blundering this. He softened his tone. "I heard about Lord Oxnard and thought..."

"So, you followed me? What do you think is going on?" There was a slight tinge of her hurt in her voice.

"It wouldn't be the first time you ran away from me. I'm just trying..."

She pulled away, took a step back, and crossed her arms. "What is it that you want from me?"

He stepped closer. "Why was my grandfather comforting you just now?"

"Are you really that naïve, that self-centered, that you cannot possibly understand how difficult this is on me?"

"Is that why you ran away earlier?"

"I already told you everything..."

Desperation consumed his words. "Why won't you just talk to me?"

Sabina looked up at him. "Why can't *you* just be satisfied with being reunited with your family?"

"I can't. I need to know. My whole life, I thought the man who died protecting us was my father, convinced myself my mother had died in childbirth, and believed Lucius and I had no other relatives." He ran a hand through his hair. "But none of that was true." Uncertainty encompassed her features. She pursed her lips and turned to walk away, but he took her arm, more gently this time, begging her to stay. "Please, I just want to understand. Every time I ask my mother or grandfather a question...it's clear they're hiding something."

Maximus didn't know what he expected to hear, but Sabina unleashing her fury was the last thing he would've expected. "You want to know what happened? I will tell you and then perhaps you will understand." Never breaking eye contact, she took two steps back. "So concerned for the safety of his friend, my father went with Lord March on his search for you and Lucius. Your father was not the only victim in that carriage accident."

"Sabina," he started as he reached for her, "I had no—"

She ignored his offering. "My mother blamed me, and it certainly wouldn't be..." She stopped short from whatever she was about to say. Inhaled deeply, then began again in a calmer tone. "Despite their own loss, His Grace and Lady March offered to care for me while my mother supposedly grieved my father's death."

"Do you not believe her grief was sincere?"

She let out a mirthless laugh. "They never cared for each other. They fought constantly but put on a tremendous performance for the outside world."

"I'm sorry."

"It is not your fault, and I am not sharing any of this to incur your sympathy."

"Then, why *are* you?"

"So you will let me be." She sucked in her breath and released it slowly, as if she were trying to ease the pain. Clearly so much had happened, too much heartache. "Your family was, still is, very kind to me. They continued to care for me when my own mother wanted to send me away. I will not do anything to tarnish that friendship."

What had Sabina endured? He knew about the Cursed Heiress rumors, but her anger and sorrow seemed to run much deeper than that to have been caused by some cruel gossip.

Vanilla and lavender encircled him as he took a cautious step forward. "I am not asking you to sacrifice anything, but something happened that affected you. Let me in," he whispered

Moonlight caressed her cheek. "I..." He could sense her resolve was softening. "I can't." The words were a mere murmur on the evening breeze.

"Stop pushing me away because of something that happened more than twenty years ago. You're letting the past rule and dictate your future."

He desperately wanted to take away the pain. He felt like a complete ass for the assumptions he'd made. Whenever Sabina was near he didn't always think straight, and tonight had been no exception.

"You don't know anything about what I endured." Sabina pulled sharply away. "I must rejoin the ladies. Good evening, Lord Maximus."

Maximus tossed the bedcovers to one side and attempted to find a comfortable position. He'd never had such trouble sleeping in his life. Staring up at the dark ceiling, he tried to clear his mind, but between everything that was happening with his brother and thinking about Sabina, he was not getting any rest.

"This is ridiculous," he chided himself as he left the warmth of his bed in search of clothing. He could stay in bed and toss and turn all night, or he could peruse the library.

The halls were dark and quiet, only the soft rustling of leaves against the windows disrupting the quiet of night could be heard. By the time he reached the library, he had decided Shakespeare's sonnets would sufficiently put him to sleep. He'd never understood the popularity of the playwright but had also never dared to voice his opinion around so many who clearly adored his works.

As he entered the library, the warm flowery scent of vanilla and lavender jarred his senses to life. His body instantly knew who was present while his mind denied what his heart had already decided.

Sabina was curled up on one of the sofas, soft candle light cascaded across her delicate cheek. At the sound of his footsteps, her head raised. Her eyes held a dreamy, far-off look. Maximus did not believe he was a romantic, but in that moment, he swore his heart skipped a beat at the sight of her.

"Good evening, Sabina." He did not want to even attempt to be correct and formal. They were past that point. He wanted to know her, be on intimate terms. From the moment he met her, he knew they were meant to be more.

"It's practically morning." The words were short and curt. She closed her book and started to stand.

"Please don't leave. I just want to talk." Maximus strolled to the sofa and took a seat beside her. "I want to apologize for what happened on the balcony. I should have never—"

"You were right. I do push people away, but too many things have happened. I'm tired..." her words trailed off and she quickly changed the subject. "Are you having trouble sleeping?"

"Yes. I never had this problem before, but now I find that in the quiet of the night, my mind is completely awake."

A chuckle escaped her lips. "Welcome to my nightly routine."

"Why do you have trouble sleeping?"

She sucked in her breath as if preparing to reveal a secret, but kept silent. He wished she would reveal so much more of herself. He didn't know what more to say to gain her trust.

"Sabina, please let me in. I won't betray your trust."

She stared at him for what felt like hours. He could sense her struggle, see it in her eyes. He meant what he said, he would never do anything to harm her. Her shoulders sagged as if carrying the weight of the world.

The words began, so quietly at first, "Ever since my father died, I've been plagued with nightmares."

Sadness seeped into his heart. Both their fathers had been taken far too soon. "I'm sorry you lost him."

"It's not your fault."

He knew it wasn't his fault, he'd been just an infant, but it still didn't diminish his guilt. The silence lingered between them. "You must miss him."

Much to his surprise, Sabina chuckled. "Yes, so much. He made me feel...." He waited in anticipation. "Safe."

"Safe?"

A delicate blond curl caressed her cheek as she nodded. "When my father was alive, I felt loved, safe, protected. After he..." Her words died off as she glanced away, sorrow weighing her features.

Maximus edged closer. He wanted her to know she was safe with him, that he would protect her. "What happened?"

She stared at him, the struggle still apparent in her eyes, before exhaling a long breath. "My mother blamed me for everything. Any time something bad happened, she threatened to send me away to some distant relative. I lived in constant fear of being removed from the only home I'd ever known because of Mother's phobia about my eyes."

His hand went to her cheek as if of its own accord and tucked an errant curl behind her ear. He studied her features, the way the candlelight danced across one brown eye and into the green.

"Were you born with two different colored eyes?"

Her eyes drifted down, studying the book in her hand. "Yes, and it truly has been a curse for as long as I can remember."

"I don't think it's a curse." Her eyes flew open and met his. "You are the most beautiful, fascinating woman I've ever known." His heart thundered with each word he spoke.

"Maximus." His name came out a breathy whisper that melted his heart. "I don't think this is a wise idea."

"Sabina, why won't you reveal yourself to me?"

She took in a sharp breath. "There's nothing more to say."

"Perhaps not in words," Maximus said as he pulled her into his embrace and kissed her.

The book she'd been holding fell to the floor as she melted into his arms. One hand cautiously explored his chest, but she did not push him away. Instead, her hand continued its exploration, igniting the flame that had always been present between them since their first meeting.

He slowed the kiss before resting his forehead on hers. "I've been wanting to kiss you since the night at the theatre."

She pulled back and looked into his eyes. Doubt and hope mixed in her eyes, mirroring her question. "You have?"

"Yes." He claimed her lips again. Words were not enough to express what he felt. The kiss turned fiery, full of need. His heart hammered in his chest as his mind fought to reason. It was the middle of the night and they were alone in the library. Anyone could walk in.

Sabina must have had the same thought. She gently broke the kiss and whispered, "I should be retiring."

Maximus watched as she left the library. He sank into the sofa's cushions, resting his head on its back. His path was clear.

Chapter Nine

MAXIMUS GRABBED HIS sketches and headed to Grandfather's study. It was quickly becoming his favorite room at Warrington Hall. It reminded him of Grandfather St. Alban's library—warm and personal and filled with mementos.

"You look like you're in quite the rush," Sabina's voice halted his progress.

She was reading in the alcove, the morning sunlight kissing the dimples on her cheek. He strolled to her side and sat beside her.

"Grandfather is going to show Lucius and me some of Father's drawings."

A slight giggle escaped her lips.

"What's so funny?"

"I just remembered an incident with our fathers." She laughed into her hand. "Your father was so excited to share his sketches, and he was furious when my father would not take any of them seriously."

"I heard my father was not a draughtsman."

"No." She brushed her hand across his. "But he was a wonderful person and passionate about everything he set his mind to."

It was a change to have Sabina willing to recount stories, rather than run away. "Thank you for telling me." He leaned forward and brushed a soft kiss across her lips inhaling vanilla and lavender which set fire to his already rising desire.

"I think you better join your grandfather before you get into trouble."

"If I get into any trouble, it will only be because you inspire me to do so."

Sabina leaned forward and kissed him soundly on the lips. "You're incorrigible." She didn't wait for a retort but got up and strolled away.

For a brief moment he thought to go after her, but he was reluctant to keep his grandfather waiting. Since arriving at Warrington Hall, they'd begun to form a special bond.

Without further delay, he headed toward the study. When he reached his destination, Grandfather had just begun to open the large leather folio on his desk. Lucius was at Grandfather's side, ignoring Maximus's entry.

"Perfect timing, Maximus," Grandfather greeted with excitement. "Come, come my boy."

He took the spot across from Grandfather and watched as he pulled out several dozen sheaves of paper and spread them across the desk. The sketches were simplistic in execution, lacking any detail, with an abundance of scribbled notes strewn across the page.

"Father's lack of talent with drawing rivals mine," Lucius said with a mocking tone.

"Perhaps not quite as bad," Maximus playfully said, attempting to ease some of the tension. He sifted through a couple of drawings before admiring one in particular. "He was not very good at sketching, but his vision certainly comes through. Look at this one."

"It was the last sketch he did…" Grandfather's voice cracked as he brushed his fingers across the paper. "He was planning to build a new orangery."

Maximus then pulled one of his sketches out of his own small folio. "I designed something similar."

Grandfather took the drawing from Maximus. "Amazing. Your skill is far superior, but the vision is quite the same."

Lucius's eyes bore into Maximus at the praise. Thankfully, Grandfather was too absorbed in the drawings to notice.

Lucius did not even attempt to be civil. "I will leave you two to discuss the *drawings*," he said before he stormed from the room.

"Tsk, tsk," Grandfather muttered. "Just like his uncle, that one. Let's not have him spoil our time." And that was all the older man said on the subject of Lucius. Once again, he turned his attention to the sketches before him. "The similarities..." his words trailed off as he intently studied the sketch of the orangery. "Have you ever executed one of your designs?"

"No. It's always been a dream, but—"

"Well, my boy," Grandfather started as he slapped his hand on the desk. "Let's make that dream a reality."

"What are you saying?" Anticipation soared through Maximus's veins.

"I want you to design the new orangery. Your father had started the project, and I want you to complete it."

A range of emotions—too many to name—soared through Maximus's body. His dream had just been handed to him and he was...speechless. Grandfather's eyes got larger, waiting for his response.

Seconds passed before he could find the words. "I...I would be honored."

Grandfather rounded the desk and wrapped his arms around him. Emotion choked his words. "Your father would be so proud."

This world, this life, was more than Maximus had ever expected, and he would cherish every moment he could spend with his grandfather. He'd just strolled back into the house after a quick walk about the garden when he spotted his brother and uncle deep in conversation, disappearing into the Bernini gallery.

Odd. Maximus doubted the pair were going in to admire the numerous sculptures. The distrust he felt from the moment he'd met his uncle had not diminished. If anything, it had grown.

He crept down the hall, careful to stay out of sight. The door to the gallery was slightly ajar. Under normal conditions he wasn't one for eavesdropping, but his brother's behavior of late had been anything but normal. He pressed closer, trying to capture their conversation.

"Thinking about all you could have?" Maximus recognized his uncle's voice.

"It is natural under the circumstances."

"What is it that *you* want?" Uncle Daniel's tone taunted Lucius.

"To have the respect of my peers and be feared by servants. To have the power to do as I please."

A disturbing chuckle drifted into the hall. "I believe you and I are more similar than you might imagine. After your father passed, I claimed my spot as heir, but with your return, I find myself reduced to third in line with no hope of greater glory." There was a long silent pause. "You would like to be the old man's heir, wouldn't you?"

"Yes."

His uncle's tone turned more carefree. "I'd like to help you become the chosen one."

"Why would you do that?"

"Because you and I are the same. I was the forgotten second son, born ten minutes too late." No one had mentioned that their father and uncle were twins. "I'm sure you always came in second through the years, and I would also venture to say Maximus has always been seen as the more stable, dependable brother." As if the brothers had not been at odds enough lately, Uncle Daniel was fueling the hatred festering in Lucius.

Maximus's blood began to boil. He wanted to barge in and confront his uncle, but soft footsteps followed by chatter signaled someone was approaching. Better not to cause a scene. He needed to figure out how to best handle this situation before he lost his head and pushed his brother further away. The last thing he wanted was to lose his brother.

Sabina was not interested in painting pretty landscapes for the sole purpose of earning praise from the gentlemen in attendance. After making her excuses about her aching head, she slipped away from the ladies, taking the shaded footpath. No one really seemed to take notice when she claimed illness anyway. Besides, all she wanted to do was lose herself in thoughts of Maximus.

She still couldn't believe he'd kissed her; just the thought of his lips on hers stirred the butterflies in her stomach to life. Maximus was everything she had dreamed of leading up to her first season, when she'd still had hope and was so naïve about the world and just how cruel it could be.

It was different with Maximus. He wasn't offended by her intelligence or scared off by her eyes. On the contrary, he seemed just as enthralled with her as she was with him.

A heavy sigh escaped her lips. She knew it wouldn't last. He was the grandson of a duke and was expected to choose an appropriate bride; a young bride who could bear future dukes. But she desperately wanted this short time with him. Sabina shuffled her feet, kicking up some dirt in the process, not caring if the dust collected on her skirt.

"Is something the matter, Miss Teverton?"

She whipped around and came face to face with crystal blue eyes and a handsome face, but not the one she desired.

"Not at all, Lord Lucius." The spot between his brows crinkled, just the same as his brother's had when she'd first called him by name. But even with that simple gesture, she could still tell the difference between them. Lord Lucius had a subtle arrogance that was always present. She suspected it was not a new trait, but a subconscious one. Not to mention, he quite frequently dressed in black, as he did today. She answered his unspoken question. "It's the pitch of your voice. It sounds different than your brother's."

He brushed off her response as he sauntered toward her. "Right from our first meeting, I thought you were quite intelligent. And now you have proven me correct."

Sabina didn't know if it was a compliment meant for himself or for her. "Thank you," she said with some hesitation. "What are you doing here? I thought the men had all gone for a ride to see the location for the new folly."

"I was prepared to join them, but then I saw you walking down the path and decided you would be much better company." He offered his arm. "It is quite a pleasant afternoon for a walk. Please allow me to escort you to wherever you were heading."

She really did not need an escort, especially with the brother she had no romantic interest in. She suspected Lord Lucius was used to having women fawn all over him, but this was one woman who would not indulge his ego.

Taking a step back, she started, "I do apologize Lord Lucius, but I feel a headache beginning and—"

"Please." With a dramatic sweep of his arm, he brought his hand to his heart. "I could not live with myself if something happened and I was not there to assist you."

Sabina was no simpering miss and did not require his assistance in the slightest, however, something told her Lord Lucius was not going to take no for an answer. So much for a quiet walk alone with her thoughts.

"Thank you, Lord Lucius. I appreciate your concern." She took the offered arm.

The lovely day was a direct contrast to what she was feeling on the inside. Within less than a few minutes, Lucius had chased away all the excited butterflies.

Although they might look identical, Maximus and his brother were nothing alike in character. Her impression was confirmed a moment later when Lucius edged closer and placed his gloved hand over hers, keeping her hand firmly on his forearm. His index finger began to move in small circles, a motion she suspected was meant to entice, but which had no effect on her.

"Will you be attending the masquerade this evening?"

"It is my intention." The annual Warrington masquerade ball had always been a favorite. It was the one time of year where she could hide her identity and pretend to be someone other than the Cursed Heiress.

"Then please do me the honor of reserving a dance."

"Only if there's room on her dance card after I've claimed mine." A warm voice entered her soul, stirring the butterflies back to life.

Sabina turned around looking for the source of the voice. In the short distance, through the branches, she saw Maximus. He looked like a god sitting atop a beautiful chestnut mare, her coat shimmering in the afternoon sunlight.

"Hello brother." Lucius's tone was none too welcoming. There was a palpable tension between the brothers. "I didn't expect you to join us."

"Mother informed me that Miss Teverton had taken ill and I wanted to ensure it was nothing serious."

Maximus was concerned for her! *Oh my.* Her stomach somersaulted with excitement. Suddenly her day did indeed seem brighter. "It's just a slight headache."

"That is very good news," he said as he dismounted his horse. She couldn't take her eyes off his magnificent form. As usual, he was wearing a blue coat that brought out the color of his eyes.

Lord Lucius's face turned red, his features narrowing on his brother with a sneer of disapproval. "I believe Grandfather may need my assistance when he returns from the ride." He faced Sabina and brought her gloved hand to his lips. "I shall think of no one else until our dance this evening."

Somehow Sabina was able to contain her laughter until Lord Lucius had disappeared down a connecting path.

"My, your brother is becoming quite the rake." The words exited her mouth with laughter.

"*Is* becoming? Let's not talk of him." Maximus pulled her into his embrace and brushed soft kisses across her cheek. "I've dreamed of kissing these dimples all day."

"And you are no better, Lord Maximus," she said with a breathy tease. "Someone may see us."

With a rakish half smile, he said, "And that would be bad?" He continued to brush kisses along her jaw, making her wish they were not out of doors where gossipmongers lingered beyond the branches. The kisses were tender, intimate, and she did not want it to end.

The sound of hooves pounding the ground in the distance brought them back to reality. "Sounds like the men have returned. I best be heading back." As he stroked her cheek, he looked deep into her eyes, never flinching. There were no barriers, no curse, no age difference, just them.

In that moment she realized just how far she'd fallen in love. Reaching up, she kissed him gently on his lips. "You may have all my dances."

From the moment Maximus had first embraced Sabina at the theatre, he'd been fascinated with her, but over the past weeks, that fascination had deepened. Without a doubt, he knew he wanted to spend the rest of his life with her. A chuckle escaped his lips. Perhaps he was a hopeless romantic after all.

He'd had little interaction with married couples through the years, but he was enthralled with the idea of experiencing all life had to offer with one woman, to have children, and grow old together. Only once had Grandfather St. Albans mentioned his late wife. He'd spoken of her with such admiration and love. Maximus knew he wanted that too. It was well within his reach with Sabina. He rounded the slight bend to where he left his horse, Mars, and came face to face with his brother.

"Let's see who the more deserving of heirs is."

Maximus had never seen his brother in such a state of anger. No, anger was too mild a word for what was coursing between them. And he knew exactly on whom to place the blame. He stood his ground, waiting for his brother to confess what his motive was.

Lucius puffed out his chest, his arms flung wide open as his head went back. A tremendous growl rumbled from his gut, echoing off the trees. "Afraid to fight me?" he taunted Maximus with a sneer.

Clearly Maximus's initial tactic was not going to get him anywhere. Best get straight to the point. "Does this have something to do with Uncle Daniel?"

"No." The single word was not convincing, but before Maximus had a chance to respond, his brother was charging toward him.

Maximus braced himself for the contact as Lucius came barreling toward his mid-section. The second their bodies met, anger and rage collided. Maximus struggled to keep his footing before they both tumbled to the ground. Lucius climbed on top of him and swung his fist with proficient force, making contact with Maximus's jaw.

Maximus ignored the pain ricocheting across his face as he fought to change positions. He thrusted the palm of his hand upward, straight into Lucius's chin.

"You bastard," Lucius growled as he rolled off Maximus. "You always have to prove you're stronger than me," he whined as he rubbed his jaw.

"Only when my brother is threatening me and acting like a rabid wolf." Maximus stood up and stared down at his twin. "Are you going to tell me what's wrong with you and why you prefer to conspire with our uncle instead of confide in me?"

"Why don't you work it out for yourself," Lucius spat out.

"There seems to be a battle raging within you, Lucius."

"You know nothing of what is raging within me."

"Don't I? We're twins. We look alike. We used to think alike, but you feed the evil within, stirring anger and jealousy."

"And you are the good twin, I suppose," Lucius's comment struck to the core of Maximus's heart.

"I never said that, but the wolf I feed does not spew lies or give into evil. I choose to be kind, to have hope, to find joy in the simple pleasures. And if Grandfather chooses you as his heir, I will share in your joy, not destroy it."

"That is very noble of you, Maximus, especially when you know damned well *His Grace* will choose you."

"You don't know—"

"I'm tired of living in your shadow."

"You've never been in my shadow and —"

"Like hell I haven't." Lucius took a step closer and glared intensely into Maximus's eyes. "You have always been favored. Always. It is my turn. I want to do as I please. I want to have no cares, and the money to do whatever I want."

"You want? You sound like a spoiled child rather than a man."

"I am a man, a man who should be, no, *will* be, the next Duke of Warrington."

"Do you honestly believe that being a duke comes with no responsibility and an endless coffer? And besides, you know damn well it is not up to you."

A sinister gleam flashed in his brother's eyes before it was masked behind a composed façade. "We shall see."

"What is that supposed to mean?"

His voice had taken an eerie calmness. "It means we will simply have to wait."

Maximus didn't know what to say to talk some sense into his brother. It had become a constant obstacle. They used to be close, they used to know each other's thoughts without saying a single word, they used to respect one another, but now...now it was as if he didn't know the person who looked so much like him standing two feet in front of him.

"I am tired of trying to talk sense into you. Ever since —"

"Yes, I know, discovered we're the heirs to the Duke of Warrington." His brother's snide tone did not sit well with him.

"No. It started well before we learnt of our heritage. This..." He pointed his finger at his brother then to himself. "This tension between us began when Grandfather St. Albans took ill and our future became uncertain."

Lucius turned his back on Maximus, refusing to look at him as he spoke. "You're wrong. This has nothing to do with him, and everything to do with the happiness you're trying to steal from me."

Maximus tried to reach out to his brother. "Don't you understand? Happiness doesn't lie with how much money you have, or what title has been bestowed upon you, or even how many women you've bedded—"

"When did you become so old?" Lucius snickered at him.

"Perhaps I was born old."

Chapter Ten

EVERY FAMILY IN the country had accepted the invitation to the Warrington masquerade ball. Maximus knew this was because everyone was curious about the return of the heirs. He hoped one day very soon the novelty would wear off. At the very least, the parade of eligible ladies was not as bad as in London.

The main ballroom had come to life with hundreds of candles illuminating every corner. The musicians had taken their places and begun to warm up. Soon, dancing and revelry would begin. As the masked guests flowed into the ballroom, Maximus searched for one familiar face. He didn't know what Sabina would be dressed as, or if she would try to conceal her eyes. He certainly hoped she did not. Damn, he was like a lovesick schoolboy whenever Sabina was near, and it was getting worse with each breath he took. He'd hoped for a moment to speak with his grandfather before the ball to make his intentions known, but with the late arrival of several relatives, Grandfather's time been consumed with familial obligations.

Eager ladies waited impatiently for Maximus and his brother to ask them to dance. He felt like he danced with every lady except the one he had wanted to. It was growing rather tedious. With each set, he grew more impatient. Where was Sabina?

Unfortunately, his uncle was not difficult to spot since he refused to wear a costume. He strolled through the ballroom, his chest puffed out, and a pompous smirk on his face. Clearly, he was pleased with himself, over what, Maximus did not know. After the conversation he'd overheard, Maximus kept a distant eye on the man, but nothing of concern had transpired.

"You seem distracted, my lord," Miss Colyer said, bringing his concentration back to the dance, and the uninteresting dance partner.

"Just taking in the evening." He doubted Miss Colyer would sense the lie, too self-absorbed in herself as she was.

"Oh, is this your first masquerade?" Her question was laced with pity.

Why did everyone assume that because Maximus and Lucius had been brought up in the country, quite sequestered from the *ton*, that they had not experienced these pleasures.

"No." He did not want to further entertain this conversation.

Let Miss Colyer turn her attention to Lucius. His brother was quite in his element, charming one lady after another, absorbing their attention. Just as soon as the dance ended, Maximus would deliver Miss Colyer to her chaperone and then search for Sabina.

"Thank you for the dance Miss Colyer," he said as he guided her toward her party hoping for a quick escape.

Disappointment streaked across her face. "But my lord...would you not care for refreshments...or perhaps a stroll in the moonlight?"

Maximus stopped short and glared down into the lady's conniving eyes. "No." He had no patience for title hunters. Not giving her the opportunity to reply, he took his leave in search of his heart's desire.

A short time later, cornered by a Domino across the room, he spotted the woman he'd been dreaming about all day. Her red gown shimmered in the candlelight. She abruptly turned away and began to maneuver her way through the crush with rushed movements. He followed suit, attempting to reach her side before she disappeared again.

He picked up his pace as she turned away from the crowd, toward the veranda.

"I believe you owe me a dance," he began to tease her before he noticed her tear-filled eyes behind the mask. "What's wrong?"

"It is nothing." Her body seemed weighed down with unhappiness. She started to pull away.

It tore at his heart to see her like this, but this was neither the time nor place to press the issue. He extended a gloved hand. "May I have this waltz?" She stared at his hand as if it might turn into a snake. She still seemed so unsure about them. "There's no one I'd rather dance with than you," he whispered, hoping to erase whatever hesitation she had.

She looked into his eyes. A soft smile eased her features. "You really mean that?"

"*Sì amore mia.*" Some of the hesitation faded as Sabina placed her gloved hand in his.

He desperately wished they weren't wearing gloves. He wanted to feel the softness and heat of her skin against his. He guided her to the center of the room and a moment later, the waltz began.

The dance was intimate, seductive. Maximus admired the sensuous gleam in her eyes, the feel of her body so close to his. They were meant for each other, that much he was certain, but, the past constantly came between them. The rumors were destroying her life, but he was not going to let them destroy their future.

"Meet me at the center of the maze after the final dance," he whispered as the dance came to an end.

The evening had been declared a grand success and as guests started to retire, Sabina slipped out, into the cool night air. She wanted to relish in the joy coursing through her entire body. Even her sister-in-law's spiteful words earlier in the evening about her eyes and derogatory comments about Titus's absence could not diminish her current happiness.

The crescent moon smiled at her as she strolled through the garden toward the maze. Everything she believed about herself, everything she had convinced herself about her future, was so different than what she was presently feeling. When she'd danced with Maximus, a thousand and one emotions she'd never experienced—never thought she would experience—had enveloped her entire being.

The path leading to the entrance of the maze was flanked by rose bushes, their sweet smell dancing across the land on the evening breeze, guiding her toward her dream. She entered the maze, taking the familiar winding path that led to its center and Vesta's folly. Seconds later, she heard soft footsteps following her deeper into the maze. Turning down a side path, she waited, hoping.

"Sabina." A deep whisper mingled with the breeze. The breath caught in her throat as he emerged from the shadows.

Maximus. Her heart skipped as his name danced across her heart. There were so many things her heart wanted to reveal, but cautiousness prevailed. She might be in love with him already, but she was not a fool.

He walked straight toward her, pulled her into his embrace, and kissed her with a hunger that seemed to match her own desire. It was not a soft kiss, but one full of need. She parted her lips, wanting to experience all he was offering. His tongue traced the curve of her lips before claiming what she was willingly giving. Pressing her body more firmly against his, she ran her fingers through his thick brown hair.

"Oh God, you are *magnifico.*" The words rumbled from his chest. "*Sei bellissima.*"

His lips skimmed her skin, setting her on fire with each inch they covered, and when he reached her ear and nibbled softly, Sabina thought she would collapse from pleasure right there and then. She'd only ever dreamed of a moment like this with him, never quite believing it could be reality.

One hand weaved down her back, bringing her closer still, his hardness a direct contrast to her soft curves. She wanted to feel more of him but knew the danger in that want. Knew the danger her heart was in. Reality could be cruel and unforgiving at times.

The kisses slowed, became more sensual, more intimate, drugging her into euphoria. Time stood still while they were in their own garden paradise. But even as the passion rose, reality was fighting its way to the forefront of her mind. There was something she had to know.

"Why are you here?" she whispered against his lips. "I mean, you could be the next Duke of Warrington, and yet you are here with me when you could have any woman, a younger woman. A woman who..."

"I don't want *any* woman. I want you. *Ti voglio.*" Her heart turned over in response. "You intrigue me more than any woman ever has." He kissed the tip of her nose. "Plus...you know *me.*" He brushed a soft kiss across her lips. "Would it bother you if I wasn't the next duke?"

"Not at all. I want you to be exactly who you are, especially with me. You are not a twin, who looks like his brother. To me, you are Maximus. You are a caring man." She cupped his cheek. "I hear it in your voice when you speak with Miss St. Albans or your mother. I see how the servants come to you, respect you. You are a good man, and much wiser than your twenty-three years would suggest."

"I think you flatter me too much."

"I think I could flatter you more."

Their brief interlude in the maze had ended all too soon. Despite all the wonderful things Maximus had said, and the way he made her feel, Sabina still had her doubts. She was seven years older than him after all and then there were the secrets she'd locked away, hoping never to have to reveal.

She paced outside the door for several minutes wondering if this was the right decision. True, Sylvia was her dearest friend, but she was also the mother of the man she was desperately in love with after all. However, she needed advice before this went any further. Before her heart was too broken to be mended. She feared she was already past that point.

She raised and lowered her hand several times before she finally knocked on the door. A moment later the door opened. "Sabina, what's wrong?" Sylvia said as she ushered her into her room and over to the settee near the fire.

"I...I don't know what to do." She worried her hands in her lap. Perhaps this was a mistake. It was far too awkward to talk to Sylvia about this.

"Dearest," Sylvia's tone softened, "What's troubling you? You know you can tell me anything."

Sucking in a deep breath, she let the words storm from her mouth before her bravado faded. "I've never felt this way before, not even with Lord Oxnard, but I'm so much older. What if I can't have children? He has to have an heir. And then there's my eyes. What if I *had* children and they had the same affliction? And then there's the kidnapping and what happened in the garden and—"

Sylvia halted Sabina's tirade with a calm tone. "Are you speaking of Maximus?"

She looked into Sylvia's caring eyes. "Yes. I...I'm in love with him. And...and I think he might feel the same."

"Oh dearest, that is wonderful news!"

"But—"

"No, no buts. This *is* wonderful." Her smile broadened in approval. "Being in love is wonderful. There are always going to be obstacles. Nothing is ever perfect. Don't let a number destroy your chance at happiness."

"But I'm seven years older than Maximus."

Sylvia clasped Sabina's hands within her own. "Take it from me, it is just a number. It doesn't mean anything. What matters most is that you love each other."

"What do you mean 'take it from you'?"

"I was two years older than my dearest Martin. I was so in love with him." She giggled like a debutante in her first season. "I think I fancied myself in love with Martin the moment we met." That was exactly how Sabina had felt about Maximus! "Daniel, however, was none-too-pleased. He also tried courting me, but I had already set my cap on Martin, although I was too shy to say anything to him. I frustrated my mother so much during my first season. I wanted nothing to do with the marriage mart, dances, outings...nothing. I knew in my heart of hearts that Martin and I were always meant to be together."

"Did he feel the same at first?" Since that night at the theatre, Sabina had often wondered if love at first sight was real. The rapid flutters in her stomach told her it was.

"I think so." Sylvia paused a moment, the spot between her brows crinkling slightly before her eyes widened. "No, I know he did." She giggled. "He was so upset with me during my first season that he barely spoke to me. He claimed it was because I had become quite the gossip. Which as you well know is not true." If Sabina knew anything of her dearest friend was that she was the furthest thing from a gossip. "He was behaving so abominably that his father sent him away."

"For how long?"

"Three years."

"That is such a long time to be apart."

"I thought so too," Sylvia confessed. "But when he returned, we were inseparable." Sadness lingered in her voice. "Although he was taken from me much too soon, I wouldn't change our time together. I couldn't imagine being married to anyone else."

Sabina did not doubt Sylvia's love for her husband. Never once had she expressed interest in anyone else after his passing. To have a love like that was more than Sabina had ever hoped for and here she was standing on the precipice wondering if she was strong enough to take that leap of faith.

"Don't let love slip away." Sylvia patted her hand. "May I offer some advice?"

"Of course." She needed some advice, along with words of encouragement, and reassurance that no matter what, it would all turn out well.

"You need to tell Maximus everything that happened the night of the kidnapping *and* the consequent events, otherwise it *will* come between you sooner or later."

Sabina didn't know if she were strong enough to confide all that. "I...I'm scared."

"I know you are dearest," Sylvia said with a sympathetic smile. "But once you tell him, you will be glad you did."

She wasn't so sure. She'd spent the last twenty-three years burying those memories, trying to escape the pain and guilt.

"Just think about what I said."

"Thank you." She reached across and hugged her dearest friend before departing.

Sabina left Sylvia's room feeling scared and unsure. She pondered everything Sylvia had said and knew deep down, she was right. Maximus deserved to know the truth, and she would have to accept the consequences.

She started toward Maximus's room, but then changed her mind. The hour was late, and it simply was not appropriate to knock on his door.

By the time she reached her room, her insides were all knotted. Could this really wait till morning? What if he rose early? Then she would miss her chance to speak with him. This couldn't wait. She stepped away from her door and took two steps before changing her mind again.

"I can't do this." She closed her eyes, then allowed her head to fall back. "This is ridiculous."

"What's ridiculous?"

"Maximus." She jumped at the sound of his voice. "Wh...what are you doing here?"

"I went to say goodnight to Mother and she mentioned you wanted to speak to me." The spot between his brows crinkled. "She implied it was rather urgent."

Sabina didn't know whether to thank her friend, or cry. "Yes." This was going to be more difficult than she thought. "I need to tell you something." Her tone sounded ominous even to her own ears.

He motioned down the hall. "The library or —"

"No." She knew it was quite inappropriate to ask him to her room, but she couldn't risk prying ears hearing what she was about to reveal. She couldn't risk the gossip. Motioning toward her room she said, "This won't take long." *And then you'll walk away forever.*

She stepped away from him and trudged the last couple of steps. Eau de Cologne encircled her, signaling that he followed close behind. Thankfully he didn't say anything.

Even once they were behind closed doors, he continued to keep silent. He approached her, almost with caution. She wrapped her arms about herself as she turned away, her heart heavy with fear.

Focusing her gaze on the flames quivering in the hearth, she peeled off her gloves, then fiddled with them. How did one confess it was all their fault?

"Sabina?" She saw his shadow on the wall sharpen as he approached.

"Please...please don't say anything," she whispered, keeping her back to him. She couldn't bear to look at him when she revealed the truth. "I have to tell you something." She swallowed hard. "You and Lucius were not alone in the nursery the night you were taken. I was there, too."

"You were there?" Shock and surprise filled his words. "You were in the room when the night nurse was murdered?"

"Yes." Her breath came in short spurts as the horrors from that night played over and over in her mind. "I woke up and she...she was dead, and you and Lucius were gone."

A gentle hand cupped her shoulder. "Oh, Sabina, I—"

Shaking her head, she said, "There's more." This...this was when she would lose him forever. "Everyone searched for weeks, never giving up hope. I spent much time with your mother during those dark hours. One day, we were reading in the garden and she got called away." The image of a young girl enjoying the first sunny day in weeks flashed in her mind. Sylvia, or as Sabina called her back then, Lady March, had given her a new parasol. "I went for a little stroll, twirling my parasol over my shoulder." She stared into the flames. "I heard voices." She had been paralyzed with fear as the voices had neared. Anxiety and dark fear bubbled to the surface, the scream building.

"Sabina," a gentle soothing voice called to her, bringing her back to the present. A blanket of warmth enveloped her. She leaned back, feeling...safe. "Shh, you don't need to say anything."

She looked down, realizing the warmth was Maximus holding her. She struggled out of his embrace and took several steps forward, still keeping her back to him. Wiping the tears from her face, she said, "You have to know. It was all my fault!" The words echoed in the room.

"It wasn't—"

"Yes, it was!" She whipped around. "I heard voices talking about the twins being held in Colchester. I told my father." She forced the words through heavy sobs. "*Your* father and mine left that very afternoon because of what I overheard. They left and never came back because of me!"

He grabbed her by the shoulders. "Sabina." His voice was firm and unwavering. "It was not your fault. Stop reliving the past."

"Don't you understand..." She gulped hard, hot tears slipping down her cheek. "Things might have been different. Your father...my papa..." She looked into his blue eyes and whispered, "They could have lived if not—"

"You don't know that for certain. No one could foresee the outcome." His words were so calm, understanding, his strength unwavering. "Sabina," he started as he lifted her chin, "I love you."

She had waited her whole life to hear those words. She regretted not saying them to her father as he'd left that sunny afternoon. But she regretted saying them even more to her mother. And then there was Lord Oxnard. Oh, how she regretted opening her heart to him. Her body ached with so much pain that she could not speak, or deliver what she desperately wanted to say.

"Let go of the past. It was not your fault." He kissed her forehead. "Let me be your future." He brushed a soft kiss across her cheek.

His warm masculine scent enveloped her. She leaned in, so tired of denying what she truly wanted. She took in a long deep breath and took a leap of faith.

"I know what I feel in my heart, but the words...they're not easy for me to speak."

Maximus's voice turned husky. "Then show me."

His words surprised her and sent a rush of warmth straight down to her toes all at once. From their first encounter, there had seemed to be a sleeping passion waiting to be stirred. She still didn't quite believe the future could be so bright after so much darkness, but for the chance to experience life with Maximus, it was worth the risk.

Standing on tiptoe, she touched her lips to his, caressing his mouth. What started as a gentle exploration quickly turned urgent. Their clothes practically melted away with the heat of desire. Maximus was perfect in every way. A surge of excitement tingled through her fingers. Slowly, she edged around his body, running her hands up his back, across his shoulders, exploring every inch of his masculine torso.

She brushed her hand across his smooth birthmark, reveling in the feel of his firm chest. She leaned in, inhaling his cologne, kissing his chest, running her tongue up the column of his neck. A moan resounded from deep in his chest. In the next moment, his mouth covered hers hungrily, erasing every doubt she'd ever had. He swept her into his arms and carried her to the bed.

Gently he laid her on the bed. Warmth emanated from him as he lowered his own body. Her soft curves molded into his lean contours. His lips seared a path down her neck to the pulsing hollow at the base of her throat awakening her soul.

The lovemaking that followed was unlike anything Sabina ever thought possible. Maximus was gentle, tender...loving.

There was no age difference. There was no curse. There were no more secrets. There was just love.

Chapter Eleven

THE MORNING MIST had given way to filtered sunlight. Although sporadic clouds dusted the sky, it was beginning to look like a splendid day. The gentlemen had taken their leave in preparation for a ride across the Warrington estate, while the ladies had begun to gather on the terrace for the picnic and games on the west lawn.

As ladies paired up and strolled along the pathway to where the afternoons festivities were to be held, Sabina walked down one of the less occupied paths, lost in recollections of a pleasurable night spent in Maximus's arms. They made love, they talked, they shared their hopes and dreams. Never in her life had she experienced such pleasure, such closeness, such intimacy.

"I don't give a bloody damn who hears." The harsh words echoed through the trees interrupting her musings.

Oh, no. She knew the brothers had been at odds as of late, but now they were bringing the argument in full view of the guests and gossipmongers.

Through the trees, Sabina could see the outline of two men. She squinted her eyes to focus on... *oh my, they're both shirtless.* Muscles glistened in the sunlight as they circled each other. This would certainly attract attention.

"You are being ridiculous. I have not tried to sway anyone's opinion against you."

"You know that's not true." Lucius's voice rose above the sounds of nature.

"It is not up to you."

"And—"

"And, it is not up to me either," Maximus growled.

Lucius charged Maximus, making contact with his mid-section, sending him flying to the ground with a thud, dirt splattering from the impact. In one swift movement, Maximus was back on his feet and storming his brother. He swung his fist, making contact with the side of Lucius's jaw. Lucius's head whipped back. He turned his full wrath on Maximus. Even from this distance, Sabina could tell Lucius's eyes were full of anger and hatred.

"All this should be mine."

"What did he say?" Lady Beatrice asked in a hushed tone as she inched closer.

Sabina glanced around and noticed the brothers had attracted quite a bit of attention. The last thing she wanted to do was reveal the source of the conflict the brothers were having. "I am not quite certain." She hoped her fib would suffice.

The small crowd of ladies grew larger as sounds of the fight rippled through nature. Gasps and curiosity escalated the tension. There must be something she could do. Out of the corner of her eye, she saw Sylvia running, concern weighing down her features. She had suffered so much, it must be tearing her apart to see her sons fighting.

Pushing past curious onlookers, Sabina made her way through the brush and ran between the brothers moments before Lucius could execute another punch, holding her hands wide. "Stop this." She looked at Lucius and then at Maximus. "Please stop," her voice softened, and then she spoke in Italian, knowing no one else would understand. "Don't you see what this is doing to your mother? And, your grandfather, he deserves more than this."

Maximus's gaze drifted over Sabina's head, settling on Sylvia. His hands fell to his side as he took a step back.

Lucius hesitated a moment longer before he followed suit, but his eyes were still filled with hatred.

The silence loomed between the brothers like a heavy mist.

Sylvia rushed to Sabina's side, while Picus began to usher the ladies away from the scene, but several lingered just beyond earshot, clearly hoping to gain a better view of the shirtless brothers.

Picking up the shirts, Sylvia tossed them to her sons. She waited until they'd donned their clothing before turning her wrath on them. "Why must you two argue? What was this all about?"

When both Lucius and Maximus kept silent, Sylvia turned to Sabina for answers.

"I think it best if I do not get involved any more than I already have." After what she'd heard, the last thing she wanted to do was choose sides. It was not her place to interfere. The brothers needed to work through their differences.

Sylvia continued to eye both her sons as dawning set in. She put her hands on her hips and edged closer to them. "I do hope this is not about who will be heir."

Clouds moved across the sky weaving deep shadows between the trees. Anger and silence reigned. Both brothers stood their ground, waiting for the other to speak. Lucius wavered for a moment before he threw up his hands and stormed off.

Sylvia turned to Maximus, her tone none-too-pleased. "I'm going to go speak with Lucius. Is there anything you want to tell me?"

"No." The single word was firm. Sabina suspected that even if there was, loyalty to his brother came first.

"Very well then. I will have a word with you when I'm finished with your brother." And with that ominous warning, Sylvia departed.

A few curious onlookers in the distance who had been lingering on the outskirts of the copse, now left Maximus and Sabina relatively alone.

"I'm sorry you had to witness that scene." Maximus said as they began to walk toward the house. "And thank you for stopping it."

"I wish I could have done more."

He ran a firm hand through his hair. "I don't know what to do," he said on a long sigh.

"You just have to give him time."

"Why is that everyone's answer?" Frustration echoed around them. "Lucius doesn't just need time, he needs to mature." Maximus shook his head. "There's more." He sucked in a deep breath. "I overhead Uncle Daniel trying to sway and provoke Lucius's opinion against me earlier. He is at the root of Lucius's current insecurities."

"That does not surprise me."

"What?" He stopped and looked at her.

A hawk cried overhead, the sound rippling through the leaves, settling on the shaded pathway. A cool breeze whistled, startling memories from the past.

Sabina hesitated whether to share what she knew. The last thing she wanted to be was a gossip. But this wasn't gossip, this was about saving his family. And, it might help Maximus to understand why his uncle was the way he was. "It was no secret that Lord Daniel and your father didn't always get on. Thinking back, I believe it bothered Lord Daniel that my father and yours were so close. They were practically inseparable, and had been that way since they were children."

"He was jealous over a friendship? They were brothers, nothing should—"

"Come between them? History is riddled with conflicts between brothers, beginning with Cain and Abel."

"But still they were family and—" he began to argue.

"Your father and uncle were never close." Sabina shook her head. Even as a young child visiting Warrington Hall with her father, she'd remembered the angst and animosity between the brothers.

"Why?"

"I don't really know. Perhaps it was just sibling rivalry." Some of her answers were speculation at best, just mere observations she'd made through the years. "After the tragedy, Lord Daniel changed. He stayed away for long periods of time. Warrington was so worried about him. Sylvia believed Lord Daniel felt guilty for not being able to do more to save his brother or find you and Lucius. Over the last several years, his anger had seemed to dissipate, but now that you've returned, that guilt...and jealousy has resurfaced." A sudden chill rippled down her spine. Sabina edged away from the shaded path. The warm sunlight chased away the unpleasant feeling from a moment ago.

"I don't want him to feel jealous or guilty, I..."

"Perhaps you should talk to your uncle. It may not improve the situation right away, but it could help the healing process."

Maximus pulled her into his embrace and brushed a soft kiss across her lips. "Not only are you enticingly beautiful, but incredibly wise."

Sabina thought she might swoon right then and there. She fought to keep the desire at bay. "I think it best we return to the house."

Sabina was tired of all the chatter, of ladies vying for Maximus and Lucius's attention, of being brushed aside as though she did not matter. She was thankful, however, that no one seemed to note the quiet glances she and Maximus exchanged during the course of the evening.

She paced the perimeter of the room, glancing from one table to another. Every so often she noticed Lucius shooting daggers with his eyes toward Maximus. The two brothers had barely been able to maintain civility during dinner.

Passing the settee, she noticed Miss St. Albans deep in conversation with Picus. If she didn't know better, she would believe they were smitten with each other. It would be nice if it were true. Picus was a wonderful gentleman, and Miss St. Albans quite an agreeable lady. Maximus had convinced her love was possible at any age.

"Are you enjoying yourself, Sabina?" Sylvia's sweet voice questioned as she strolled toward her.

"As much as I can." She never had fancied playing cards and always chose to watch, which could be quite tiresome.

Sylvia leaned in and whispered. "Maximus is waiting for you in the alcove near the Unicorn tapestry."

"Are you aiding your son?" Sabina was shocked she'd said the words, but even more so by Sylvia's response.

A smile teased the corner of her mouth. "To bring two people I dearly love together, of course."

"Thank you." The words rushed from Sabina's mouth before she quickly left the room.

With all the guests currently in the card room, this part of the house was not well-lit. She took her time, waiting for her eyes to adjust to the dimness. Hazy moonlight filtering in from the large window illuminated her path.

"Maximus?" she whispered his name.

He emerged from the alcove, pulling her into his arms and covered her mouth with his in an all-consuming kiss that sent a delicious jolt all the way down to her toes.

"I can't believe you enlisted your mother to aid in your seduction," she playfully slapped his firm chest.

"Neither can I, but I am most pleased with the results." He moved his mouth over hers, teasing, nibbling, enticing. In between kisses, he said, "I believe I need to sneak into your room this evening and show you what's been on my mind all day."

Oh dear. Anticipation soared through her veins as remembrance of their last time together, their naked bodies intertwined, and the way his lips kissed and explored her body.

The words rushed from her mouth with anxious excitement, "How long before you'll come to me?"

"An hour."

An hour seemed like an eternity. She didn't want to wait even a minute. "I'll be waiting."

He brushed her lips with several soft kisses before he returned to the guests. *An hour.* She would melt into a puddle just thinking about him. A walk through the hedge-enclosed rose garden before she retired should help cool her inflamed body and pass the time.

Clouds had crept across the sky, blanketing what little moonlight there was, and extinguishing the twinkle of stars. Sabina wandered to her favorite corner of the rose garden, inhaling the fragrant aromas all around her. She stood there for several minutes enjoying the quiet sounds of night.

"You're late," a deep, husky voice rippled from behind a grouping of tall hedges.

Who was that? Were two of the guests having a clandestine meeting?

Sabina began to edge away. It was none of her business who met here and for what purpose.

"I'm sorry, but..."

The sound of a young lad apologizing startled her. It wasn't a clandestine affair between two lovers, but something else. She didn't know whether to make her presence known, tip-toe away in the opposite direction, or stay put and wait for them to finish.

"I don't want excuses. Is everything we discussed ready?" The voice on the other side of the hedge sounded urgent. "I don't want anything to go wrong. I've waited twenty-three years for this."

Twenty-three years? Could this have something to do with Maximus and his brother?

"Yes, Mal—"

"I've told you before, no names. Now go, and do not disappoint me."

"Yes." A shaky whisper escaped from the young man before rushed footsteps trailed away, receding into the dark night.

Except for the intense pounding in her heart, Sabina kept perfectly silent, hoping that whoever was on the other side of the tall hedge did not come her way. Her instincts told her something nefarious had just occurred. But what proof did she have? Part of a name and the possibility that something might occur.

Panic rose from within. This was just like when... Her breath came in short spurts. Images of the last time she saw her father filled her mind as guilt weighed her down. She could not lose another loved one. She began to choke on her breath as the contents of her stomach rose within. The ground beneath her started to give way and...

Breathe. Stay calm and think, she commanded herself. *Just breathe.*

Several deep breaths later, the ground was firm, and her thoughts less hazy. She scanned her mind, trying to recall what plans had been made. A picnic was all that came to mind. Even still, she was not going to let anything to chance. The footsteps on the other side slowly withdrew. She counted to twenty before she retreated in the opposite direction, back toward Warrington Hall.

She was greeted by loud boisterous laughter ricocheting off the walls as those around tried in vain to conceal their cards. She stayed at the back of the room, hoping not to attract attention. Not wanting to alarm Maximus, who was now sitting with his grandfather, she decided she would seek Picus. He would know how to proceed...she hoped.

Chapter Twelve

MAXIMUS HAD ANOTHER tempestuous night, tossing and turning in an endless nightmare. The worst part was he couldn't remember a single detail, just the horrific feeling that something evil was lurking in the shadows, ready to strike at his happiness. Perhaps it was just his mind reacting to the conversation Sabina had overheard, but deep down he knew the truth. He prayed his twin was not at the source of this conflict.

If he were being honest with himself, he did not care which of them was named heir. He only cared that he had more family, that he knew where he came from, and that his mother and grandfather had accepted Larentia. Sadness crept into his heart once again. He only wished he'd had the opportunity to know his father.

His twin brother on the other hand had continued to become greedy in his desires. Maximus paced the length of his room several times before deciding he needed to speak with Larentia. She knew both him and Lucius best and hopefully could provide words of wisdom to guide him.

Glancing at the mantle clock, he had less than half an hour before the day's activities began. Opening the door to his room, he strolled down the hall toward the library. At this time of morning, Larentia would be completely enthralled with a book in the extensive library.

He had just reached the grand marble staircase when his progress was halted by the appearance of his brother, emerging from the opposite corridor.

"Just the person I was looking for," Lucius's words dripped with animosity. Maximus had never heard his brother take that tone, not with him, not with anyone.

"I believe it best we discuss whatever is bothering you outside." He didn't want to fuel the gossip that had begun to circulate after yesterday's fight.

"No, we will discuss it here, right now. I'm tired of waiting for the perfect time." Lucius's brows drew together in an angry frown.

"What is that supposed to mean?"

Lucius mimicked a lady's voice, "Lord Maximus is so handsome." They looked identical, but Maximus was not about to point out the obvious. His brother continued with his tirade. "Lord Maximus is in quite high demand. Lord Maximus is so much like His Grace. Lord Maximus—"

"Who is saying such nonsense?"

"Your name is on every young woman's tongue."

He was about to argue when soft chatter and laughter drifted up the staircase, halting their disagreement. He glanced down and spied several ladies conversing in hushed tones. He could only assume they were talking about him and Lucius. One of the women glanced up, giving a perfect view of her creamy neck before she tilted her head toward Miss Cornelia, stifling a giggle behind her hand.

"This is not over," Lucius growled under his breath.

"Lord Lucius, Lord Maximus," Picus greeted as he came toward them. "The gentlemen have begun to assemble on the west lawn, and your horses will be brought around fifteen minutes hence. Most of the ladies have already claimed their spots to watch the race. His Grace is preoccupied with his steward this morning but will join his guests for the afternoon festivities."

Even as Picus was explaining, Lucius had clearly lost interest, and began to head downstairs with a rapid cadence.

As usual of late, Maximus felt the need to apologize for his brother's behavior. "Don't mind him, Picus, he's..."

"Acting like a child who is not getting his way," Picus finished his sentence.

"Yes," Maximus chuckled.

"There have been a lot of changes, and even more uncertainty. Miss St. Albans informed me that this behavior is standard for Lord Lucius. I'm sure he will come around. Just give him time."

That was everyone's grand advice. *Just give him time.* How much time did Lucius need before he did something truly catastrophic? He'd given his brother plenty of *time*. After the race, he would have it out with Lucius once and for all.

Picus had started to turn away. There was at least one thing Maximus could get off his chest then and there. "Picus, a moment, please."

"Is anything the matter?" His forehead creased with concern.

It was a delicate topic. He wasn't a blood relative, but he felt responsible for his adoptive mother. He'd made a promise, after all. "I've noticed you and Larentia—"

"I apologize," Picus halted his speech. "I respect you greatly, Lord Maximus, and I should have come to you with my intentions." Maximus had never seen a man blush so fiercely. "Miss St. Albans is a remarkable woman and it would give me great pleasure if you would allow me to court her."

Over the past weeks, it was clear Picus and Larentia had formed more than a friendship. The news greatly pleased Maximus, he only wished Grandfather St. Albans was still alive. He would have approved of the match with enthusiasm, ecstatic to know that his only child would have the chance to experience what he'd had with her mother.

"You have my blessing." There was a moment's hesitation. "I only ask that you seek my brother's approval as well."

"Of course, Lord Maximus. I will speak with him after the race." Picus was positively beaming. "Thank you."

A short time later, the ladies had gathered on the veranda. Excited giggles and chatter echoed across the lawn as the gentlemen who were to participate in the race began to parade on horseback before the guests. Maximus had to hold his tongue when he saw Lucius atop Virgil. The horse was a strong, spirited creature, and no match for Lucius, in his opinion.

Maximus guided Mars to the far end of the line, incurring a spiteful gaze as he passed Lucius. It was probably for the best that Lord Spalding and Mr. Gilbert separated him from his twin.

The horses grew agitated as they awaited the start of the race. Adrenaline rushed through Maximus's veins, giving life to every inch of his being.

When the shot was fired, the horses took off at immense speed, the pounding of hooves drowning out the sound of cheers from the veranda. The course was to the end of the west lawn, round the pond, past the Roman temple, and finally a jump over a low stone wall to complete the circuit. It was a simple route, made difficult only by the number of participants.

Within the first dozen strides, Lucius pulled out ahead of the others, encouraging his horse on to greater speeds. Maximus spurred on Mars. He was not going to be bested by his brother in a simple horse race.

Lord Spalding was keeping pace with Maximus as they rounded the pond, heading toward the Roman temple. Maximus's heart was pounding in time with Mars's gait. He was half a dozen strides behind Lucius when he noticed his brother's seat was unstable.

"Damn idiot," he swore, his words drowned out by the thundering of horse hooves. He snapped the reins, urging Mars faster. He needed to reach his brother.

Seconds felt like minutes as Maximus slowly gained strides on his brother. He was only several off from Lucius as they approached the stone wall. Everything around Maximus faded as he watched his brother and Virgil in slow motion, the horse's hind legs thrusting them into the air. Moments later, the horse's front legs came down hard upon the earth, mud dispersing with the force. Lucius flew over his mount's head, landing hard on the ground.

"No!" Maximus's voice crescendoed over the sounds of horses and cheers.

Lord Spalding pulled away and slowed his horse. Maximus came to an abrupt halt, paying no heed to those around him, and rushed to his brother. Pain and anger ripped through his body. How could he have let this happen? He should have never allowed Lucius to participate in the race when he was angry.

Blood was everywhere. A large gash slashed across Lucius's face, and his body lay tangled in its own limbs. But shallow breathing gave Maximus at least some hope. He knelt down beside his brother but was afraid to touch him for fear of injuring him further.

"Lucius, what hurts?"

Lucius turned a painful gaze toward Maximus. He offered a weak contorted smile. "Everything."

"Damn it." Fear struck his core as every inch of his body ached.

An anxious crowd formed around them, suffocating Maximus, his lungs constricting. He fought for calm, trying to assess the situation. A severe pain struck through Maximus's heart. He didn't need anyone to tell him his brother's condition was serious.

Picus came running up and began to inspect Lucius. "Both his legs appear broken." His features turned mournful. "There's no surgeon nearby, but Leonard, the estate blacksmith, can set the bones."

Everything went from hectic to absolutely chaotic. Lucius was transported up to the house on a cart by several large guests. His moans of agony further adding to Maximus's distress. Maximus followed, not seeing those around him, but when a gentle hand reached for his, he knew instantly it was Sabina's.

He looked down into her dual-colored eyes. Understanding passed between them.

"Your mother and Miss St. Albans are being escorted to the drawing room. I will stay with them."

"Thank you." Without further words, they retreated to the house along with the guests. By the time they reached the entry, everyone had begun to gather in the large drawing room, anxiously awaiting any news.

Picus pulled Maximus aside. "His Grace has been notified, and the blacksmith has been summoned."

Maximus looked about the room as dozens of concerned faces met his gaze. Murmurs of speculation swirled through the room.

"Do you think Lord Lucius will live?"

"This must be so difficult for Lady March and Miss St. Albans."

"And so painful for His Grace."

Maximus searched the room for Larentia and his mother, ignoring the comments until one wretched earl said, "Lord Maximus must be pleased."

The full furry of his anger rose from his chest and spewed from his mouth. "How dare you say such foul words, you pompous ass."

"You have no right speaking—"

"No! *You* have no right." He thrust his finger at the man's chest. "You have no right to assume what I must be thinking, to assume I would be pleased by my brother's injury. You will leave this house immediately and never return."

"I don't need to take this abuse from anyone," Lord Wilkins said with haughtiness. "It's best I leave before the Cursed Heiress strikes again."

The words settled in Maximus's fist and with one strong swing, he made contact with the side Lord Wilkins' jaw. The man stumbled back, colliding with another guest.

He reached out and grasped Wilkins' cravat, lifting him from the ground. "Get out," the words rumbled from his gut.

The room hushed as all eyes turned to Maximus. Larentia appeared at his side along with his mother, concern and sadness consumed their features. He did not say another word but escorted them from the room down the hall to the small private parlor.

"I'm sorry," he said as he stretched out his hand, relieving some of the discomfort.

"I'm glad you punched him." Mother took his right hand in hers and rubbed his fingers. "Lord Wilkins *is* a pompous ass." Maximus stared at his mother, shocked that she just used such language. "He deserved far worse for what he said about Sabina."

"He's..." Loud screams raged from down the hall, interrupting his thoughts.

Mother grimaced and recoiled, her eyes filling with tears.

Maximus was about to offer comforting words when Larentia stepped beside her. "Lucius will be fine. He is strong and stubborn. It's not the first time something like this has happened."

"Really?" A mountain of hope was in that one word his mother spoke. He was thankful for Larentia's calm demeanor.

"Why don't you go and aid with your brother. I will keep Lady March entertained with tales of Lucius's misadventures," Larentia said in a calming voice that was meant for his mother, but had the same effect on him.

It was the only encouragement Maximus needed, and besides, if past experience was any indication, it would be no place for a lady while the bones were being set.

"This way, Lord Maximus," Picus guided him toward Grandfather's study. "We thought it best not to maneuver Lord Lucius upstairs at this time."

He stopped just short of the door and turned to Picus. "If you would be so kind as to find Miss Teverton and escort her to the private drawing room with Lady March and Miss St. Albans?"

"Of course, Lord Maximus."

Maximus pushed his way past the men loitering near the entrance of the study and went straight to his brother. Lucius's face was pale, almost ghostlike. His brother had managed to injure himself numerous times over the years, but this was by far the worst, tenfold.

Before he could formulate any words, Grandfather said, "He passed out from the pain. Leonard is about to set the bones."

Sucking in his breath, Maximus watched as Leonard began to set Lucius's legs. Sickening crunches filled the room. Maximus had seen and heard far worse, but the thought of his brother enduring this made his stomach turn. It was probably a good thing his brother had passed out.

No sooner had the task been completed than Uncle Daniel's voice rushed past the bystanders. "How is he?"

"Where have you been?" Grandfather's tone was almost accusatory.

"I had business to tend—"

"What could possibly be more important than your nephews?"

"It's always about your heirs, isn't it, Father?" Uncle Daniel's tone sounded much like the one Lucius had adopted over the past weeks. The hair on the back of Maximus's neck stood on end as he remembered the conversation he'd overheard in the Bernini Gallery.

Although concerning, he'd ultimately dismissed the conversation as mere jealousy and decided it best to simply talk to his uncle rather than make accusations.

Doubt settled into his chest.

Was it possible that his uncle orchestrated the accident?

No...yes...he didn't know what to think.

Grandfather's tranquil words reached his ears. "It's about family."

Uncle Daniel's eye began to twitch as his anger ricocheted through the room. "Damn it, I'm your family and you've never shown such care for me." He edged closer to the door, hands shaking fiercely. "You should have been in that carriage accident with Martin, not Lord Teverton."

Silence enveloped the room as all eyes turned toward Uncle Daniel. And through it all, Grandfather's disposition remained calm. "So, you could become the next Duke of Warrington?"

"It was never about being the next Duke of Warrington." Uncle Daniel's eyes narrowed, oozing with hatred and jealousy.

"Your Grace," Leonard interrupted. "Lord Lucius is stirring."

"We will discuss this later," Grandfather said to Uncle Daniel.

"We most certainly will." The dark tone of Uncle Daniel's voice struck at Maximus's heart.

The moment Sabina entered the house, she went to Quint, the head housekeeper, and began to make arrangements for Lucius's care. She didn't want Sylvia or Warrington worrying about anything, they had enough to occupy them at present. Once everything was finalized, she went in search of Sylvia. She couldn't imagine what this was doing to her dearest friend.

No sooner had she entered the drawing room when murmurs rippled through and all eyes settled toward her. Instinctively she knew what was about to happen but was too paralyzed with fear to run away. Sabina's insides tightened, and tears began to sting her eyes.

"It would seem the Cursed Heiress found another victim," her sister-in-law sneered from across the room, ensuring everyone heard.

Barely able to keep the emotion from her voice, Sabina pleaded, "Why do you find such joy in tormenting me, Eunice?"

"She is not trying to torment you," Sabina's mother began, "just stating the truth. Wherever there is tragedy, you are present."

No one came to her defense. No one offered any consolatory words. Quite the contrary in fact. Before long, it seemed as if everyone in the room had named someone they believed was wronged by the Cursed Heiress.

Sabina's heart crashed to the floor, breaking into a dozen pieces. This is what she'd always feared. Her worst nightmare had come true. She would always be The Cursed Heiress, and she and Maximus would never have peace.

The time had come for her to make a quiet retreat, but first there was something she must do. She'd always hoped that one day her mother might show some semblance of kindness toward her, some sort of motherly affection, but like so many of her hopes and dreams, it was time to close the book.

Marching up to her mother, Sabina took in a long steady breath. Clasping her hands in front of her to keep them from shaking, she began, "I cannot stop the gossips, however, there *is* something within my control." Her mother's mouth opened wide as if to speak, then quickly clamped it shut with an unattractive frown. "From this day forward, you and I shall no longer be family. We shall have no interaction, and no words shall be exchanged henceforth." Although her voice cracked and eyes burned with raw emotion, her spirit did feel a little lighter. Sabina walked away without giving her mother the opportunity to respond.

The clock struck half past eleven. All was quiet as Sabina snuck down the hall toward Lucius's room. She peered around the corner, ensuring the way was clear. Only the guard Warrington had placed outside Lucius's room was present. After the episode with Lord Daniel, wanting to take no chances, Warrington had placed guards throughout the house.

As she approached the door, Gerran, a footman, raised a quizzical brow.

"Is anyone sitting with Lord Lucius?"

"No, Miss Teverton. Lady March and Miss St. Albans left a few minutes ago, and His Grace and Lord Maximus should be returning shortly."

"Thank you. I won't be long," she said as she passed Gerran and opened the door.

Soft light from the fireplace cascaded across the walls, disappearing into dark corners. Restful breathing drifted from the bed. She approached with caution, unsure what to expect. Lucius lay perfectly still, only the gentle rise and fall of his chest indicated he was alive.

Uncontrollable tears streamed down her cheeks at the sight of the wide gash that started at his forehead, and had somehow narrowly missed his eye, before continuing down his cheek.

"This is all my fault," she whispered. "I pray that someday you'll forgive me for all the pain I brought you and your family."

She kissed the pad of her pointer finger and then lightly touched his forehead.

"Goodbye, Lucius."

A soft moan escaped his lips.

Sabina quickly retreated, not speaking to, or making eye contact with Gerran. Picking up her pace, she hurried to her room to gather the last of her things before departing Warrington Hall forever, off to a quiet corner where cursed spinsters could be forgotten.

Chapter Thirteen

THREE DAYS HAD passed and there was still no sign of Uncle Daniel and, to make matters worse, Sabina had disappeared. He had searched the house, the outbuildings and grounds, questioned servants, and begged his mother to reveal anything she knew. He'd dispatched several servants to aid in his search and was currently waiting—rather impatiently—for news. Lucius was the only reason Maximus had not torn apart the countryside looking for her. His condition was still precarious, and Maximus did not want to venture far.

"Lord Maximus," Picus said as he quietly strolled into the study. "Your brother is asking for you."

"Thank you."

Minutes later, Maximus entered the warm bedroom, not knowing what mood he would find his brother in today. Just because Lucius asked for him did not mean the visit would go well. He'd been sitting with his brother in between looking for Sabina, but few words had been exchanged.

Lucius rolled his head and met Maximus's gaze. Their eyes met, locked. Perhaps it was a trick of the mind, but the bond they'd always shared seemed a little more...normal.

"Thank you for visiting me today," Lucius said in a pleasant tone as he pushed himself up with his arms. "I guess people will be able to tell us apart." He chuckled as he touched the gash on his face.

"I'm sure it will heal just fine. You seem in better spirits." Relief coursed through Maximus's body. The color had returned to Lucius's face and the pain he'd worn since the accident was no longer present.

"I've had time to think."

"About?"

"All the trouble I've caused, about how far Uncle went to enact his revenge, what you said about being the grandson of a duke, how I've treated you and Larentia, and Mother, and..."

Maximus shook his head. "I am not a priest, you don't need to confess your sins."

Lucius's eyes narrowed as his expression turned serious. "But don't you see, I do. So much of this could have been avoided." He looked down the length of his legs. "*This* could have been avoided."

"You don't know that. We've always been competitive, and with the title—"

"I never wanted it." Lucius's confession took Maximus aback.

"What?"

"I never wanted it, not really. I just wanted to be the mischievous rake about town, not have any cares in the world. You're the one who wants to build, make improvements, take care of people. Uncle Daniel had convinced me that I was being purposefully forgotten, that I was not favored. He saw me as a means to get his revenge."

"And he almost succeeded." Maximus approached and gently eased on to the edge of the bed. "I would do anything to protect you."

"I know." Lucius pulled out a letter from the book on the nightstand. "I finally read the letter from Grandfather St. Albans. You were right. I was angry that he died, that we were forced to leave our home...everything."

"And you came to that revelation from reading the letter?"

"Grandfather St. Albans knew *me*, knew my faults. His words of wisdom, advice, hope for me...that's what changed my mind."

"About?"

"I want you to be Grandfather's heir."

For the second time in a short span, Maximus felt his heart constrict. "Nothing has been decided and—"

"No one knows which of us is the oldest. I am content with being the brother of a marquess, who will one day be duke." His eyes filled with admiration and love. "Who I know will *always* be there for me, despite my propensity for getting into and sometimes creating trouble." Lucius chuckled and then patted the side of his leg. "And don't think just because these don't work right now, that I will not be mischievous."

Laughter rumbled from Maximus's chest for the first time since this nightmare had begun. "Oh, I look forward to the mischief you will create, dear brother." He leaned in and embraced his twin with all the love in his heart. "It's good to have you back."

"It's good—albeit in a less than perfect form—to be back." Lucius eased himself back on the pillow.

"Grandfather was here earlier. I informed him of my decision. I believe he is most anxious to get you acquainted with your new duties as heir to the dukedom."

Several hours later, Maximus went in search of his mother. It was time to set everything to right. He walked into his mother's private parlor and sat down beside her.

She glanced up from her needlepoint. "I had a feeling you would visit me."

"I have looked everywhere for Sabina, and even sent word to her brother's house." The response he'd received from Lady Teverton was less than cordial at best. It wasn't any wonder Sabina held such qualms about her eyes and all the gossip. "Where is she hiding?" Maximus was prepared to do battle until his mother gave him the information he desired.

Gazing into the fire, Mother pondered for a moment. "When you and Lucius were taken, she was just a child. It was very difficult for her. You have witnessed firsthand how cruel the gossipmongers have been, how cruel and unloving her mother can be."

"Do you doubt my affection for her?"

"No. If I had any doubts, be certain, I would have let you know. Sabina has been more than a companion, she's been family." Mother looked pensively into Maximus's eyes. "She will need your strength to overcome years of gossip and heartache."

Maximus took his mother's hands in his. "I will protect her and love her. I will ease her fears, and hopefully with time, take them away completely. You have my word."

Pride shone bright in Mother's eyes as the full impact of his words sunk in. "She's residing at the hunting cottage on the Teverton estate."

"Thank you." He kissed his mother's cheek then quickly departed. He wasn't going to wait a moment longer.

"Lord Maximus! Lord Maximus!" The shrill, panicked sound of a young woman's voice met his ears.

He wanted to pretend he hadn't heard her, but proper manners won. Trying to hide his annoyance, he turned around and forced a smile. "Good afternoon, Miss Symlen."

"Are you leaving?" He supposed her disappointed tone and pouty lips were meant to entice, but they had the opposite effect on him.

"Yes, I have business to attend," he said with a nod, as he turned to walk away.

"Perhaps you would enjoy company?"

The only person he would enjoy the company of was currently ignoring him, but not for long. He settled for politely declining. "It would be far too tedious for someone like you. Good day, Miss Symlen."

He did not wait for a response but strode swiftly toward his destination.

As he approached Mars, the horse seemed just as anxious as he was to be set free. Within minutes he was galloping across the south lawn toward the cottage, the wind pushing at his backside, urging him toward his destiny.

The angry roll of thunder alerted him that Mother Nature would soon unleash her fury. He spurred Mars on. He wasn't familiar with this area, but he followed his mother's directions. A small stable on the back side of the pristine cottage offered protection from the weather. He quickly tended to his horse before going around to the front.

As he opened the front door, a huge gust of wind rushed past him, pushing the door wide open, slamming it against the wall. Sabina turned around. Her long wavy blond hair caressed her torso. She looked positively splendid. He was not going to give her the chance to refuse him again. He slammed the door shut, closing them in to outside world.

Sabina pulled *I Quattro Libri dell'Architettura di Andrea Palladio* from the bookshelf and strolled to the sofa, placing the book on a side table, before taking a turn about the room. Since she'd taken up residence in the cottage, she'd been reading quite a bit. Not that she minded, but she feared she would soon have nothing left to read. It wasn't a horrible place to live, she tried to convince herself as she glanced around at all the little details her brother had added for her benefit— extra bookshelves, several large comfortable chairs for reading, and their father's writing desk. The renovations were indeed quite lovely. It was just that she was lonely. She shook those thoughts away. She promised herself she would not indulge in thoughts of her previous life. If she did, she might give in to the urge to run straight back to Warrington Hall.

A large squall rattled the windows, the front door slammed against the wall, startling her senses. A moment later a large silhouette filled her doorway. Her heart thundered against her chest. In three strides, Maximus was pulling her into his embrace and kissing her with a hunger that matched her own.

The kiss bordered between sensuous and frenzy, taking and giving, a garden of pure bliss. Her entire body was instantly awakened and demanding more. Maximus raised his mouth from hers and gazed into her eyes.

"I am not letting you go."

As delicious as that sounded, her past was riddled with gossip and proof of the curse. Maximus needed a younger woman, a woman who could bear him heirs, who didn't have the stigma of a curse. She couldn't bear it if something happened to Maximus because of her. His brother's suffering still too fresh in her mind.

"But I'm the Cursed Heiress. Awful things always seem to happen—"

He halted her protests with a searing kiss, clouding her sense. Moments passed before he slowly eased back. "Sometimes bad things do happen. It's part of life, not because of you." Maximus fingered a loose tendril of hair brushing her cheek. "Lucius's accident was just that...an accident. He is recovering and will be his mischievous self in no time at all."

Sabina worried the edge of her lip. The barrier she'd been trying to build was crumbling. Could she really let go and give in to the possibility of love? She desperately wanted to.

"And I certainly hope your avoiding me didn't have to do with our age difference." His tone was light and teasing. "Age should not matter. It's just a number."

"Sylvia said something to that affect." Her earlier concerns which seemed so monumental at the time had diminished to a mere speck.

"My mother is very wise." He cupped her face. "Listen to me, Sabina. It doesn't matter how old you are or how old I am. It doesn't matter what the gossips say. It doesn't matter what happened in the past. What *does* matter is what we feel for each other." He cupped her cheek, stroking one dimple with his thumb. "Any other hesitations you would like me to discredit?"

Could she really say the words? Her chest felt as if it would burst. She lowered her gaze, a hot tear trailing down her cheek. "Maybe I should have told you sooner, but...but I was too scared."

Maximus's gentle finger raised her chin. The heart-wrenching tenderness in his gaze gave her the courage she needed. "You never have to be frightened with me."

"I'm in love with you." Every muscle in Sabina's body tightened as she braced herself for rejection.

His large warm hand took her face and held it gently. "And I'm in love with you." His eyes brimmed with passion as his mouth curved into a seductive smile. He brushed a kiss across her lips before saying, "*Ti amo.*"

"My insides melt when you speak Italian. I could listen to you for the rest of my life." Standing on tiptoe, she returned his kiss with all the urgency currently storming her body.

"*Tu sei mia.* You will always be mine." Years of worry and anxiety began to fade away with his words.

Maximus took her mouth in another searing kiss as he swept her into his arms and carried her to the sofa. Within moments, their clothes were scattered on the floor, the heat simmering between them was more intense than the fire warming the room.

With one hand, he brushed her hair away from her face as the other weaved a pattern across her chest, to the valley between her breasts. With a delicate finger, he circled the fullness of one globe, then the other, before teasing one nipple with the tip of his finger. The sigh that escaped her lips encouraged further exploration.

He leaned down and took the nipple in his mouth, alternating between licking and sucking. Sabina's fingers intertwined in his hair, bringing him closer. She savored the feeling of his hands, his mouth, his body upon hers.

"Oh yes," she sighed, never wanting the moment to end.

He shifted her position encouraging her to straddle his thighs. "I've wanted you like this for days." Her hands braced on his smooth muscular chest as she lowered herself, taking in the full length of him. "You're quite good at that," he moaned.

His hands moved gently down the length of her back, settling on her hips. Their bodies were in exquisite harmony, melting into one as they soared higher and higher. Sabina was caught up in the passion, the desire, as ecstasy spiraled through her body. When her release came, the pleasure was pure and explosive, absolutely divine.

She lay nestled in his arms, her body warm and content, his heartbeat a gentle staccato against her ears. He whispered into her hair, "*Tu sei la mia luna, il mio sole.*" She lifted her head. The smile he gave her sent her pulse racing. "*Tu sei al mia amore, mia tutto.*" He touched his lips to hers, a whisper brushed across them as he spoke. "Marry me."

Pulling back, she gazed into his eyes which held so much promise for a bright and happy future. Joy bubbled from within, releasing in a series of tears.

"Yes!"

Chapter Fourteen

THE DAY HAD started pleasantly enough. After spending time with Larentia and Sylvia in the orangery, Sabina decided to take a long walk since Maximus was touring the lands, learning estate business from Warrington. Many of the guests had departed, wanting to give the family privacy after Lucius's accident. Only a handful of relatives had remained. Those who stayed had given the family room during this tumultuous time. She was thankful for the calm and quiet, as it gave her time to reflect on the last several days.

Maximus's patience, understanding, and love never ceased to amaze her. She believed him when he said it didn't matter if he had an heir, that she mattered most. Perhaps if he'd been raised as the Duke's heir, the importance of begetting an heir himself would have been constantly ingrained in him, and Maximus would have a different mindset. She was thankful he did not. Standing under the portico of the roman temple the previous Duke of Warrington had built, Sabina enjoyed the excellent view of Warrington Hall in the distance.

The clouds began to shift, casting odd shadows on everything it touched. A fierce wind howled, disrupting her thoughts. Within moments, the clouds turned angry, a storm about to unleash its vengeance on the land. A dark cloudlike shadow gripped the side of the house with claw-like nails. A shudder rippled down her spine and straight to her toes; this was a bad omen.

Fears of the past brought her fully awake. Picking up her skirts, she started to run toward the house. Her feet propelled her closer toward Warrington Hall. The heavy morning air stung her lungs, but she did not slow her pace. After all that had happened as of late, she needed to know Maximus was safe.

Angry words echoed in the near distance. "I should have dispensed with you the moment you were discovered."

She knew that voice.

Where had she heard that voice before? She scanned her memory, narrowing down all the possibilities, until it dawned on her. The garden. It was the same voice she'd heard all those years ago when she was just a little girl. Voices swirled in her head. *Oh, no!* And it was the same she'd heard in the rose garden the night before Lucius's accident.

"How dare you threaten me." Maximus's words shot through the air, piercing her heart. She gasped, panting in terror.

Picking up her skirt, Sabina raced toward the voices. She didn't know what she would do, but she had to do something. She could not lose another loved one.

Please let Maximus be safe.

"What have you done?" Maximus demanded. He had been searching for answers for so long, but he'd never believed his uncle could truly be at the root of this evil.

Picus edged forward trying to insert himself between Uncle Daniel and Maximus and his grandfather.

"I'd stay right where you are, Picus." The icy tone in his uncle's voice warned that he was willing to do anything to enact his revenge.

Him and his grandfather stared in disbelief as Uncle Daniel weaved his tale while waving the pistol between them. "I've only tried to obtain what was rightfully mine. You see, nephew, I was the one who had you and your brother taken when you were only a few weeks old. Unfortunately, the man I hired was incompetent and didn't drown you as ordered. Instead, he tried to save you, but that plan backfired on him, since he died trying to save you. And then there was your dear father. Miss Teverton played nicely into that plan."

"It was you that day in the garden," Sabina screamed as she neared them.

What was Sabina doing here?

A sinister laugh rolled out of Uncle Daniel's mouth, filling the air.

Maximus met Sabina's gaze and gently shook his head, begging her to keep still. It was clear his uncle was not of sound mind.

Recollections of the story Sabina had told him about that fateful day twenty-three years ago when she'd overheard voices in the garden rushed to the forefront of his thoughts. "You planned for her to overhear you?"

Sabina had suffered for years because of his uncle's schemes, because of jealousy?

"How else could I have executed my design? Even while lying on that dusty stretch of road, clinging to life, Martin never gave up hope that his sons would be found." Uncle Daniel settled his gaze on Maximus and snickered. "I guess that was one thing he was correct in believing."

"You had your nephews kidnapped, and murdered your own brother?" Incredulousness seeped from Grandfather's words, as he took a step closer to Uncle Daniel.

"I never laid a hand on Martin." He was quick to declare his innocence. "It was a carriage accident and nothing more. No one could prove otherwise."

"You might as well have strangled him with your bare hands the guilt is so thick." The angry words rumbled from Grandfather's throat. "And for what? To become a duke?"

Uncle Daniel shook his head. "It was never about becoming the next Duke of Warrington."

"Then, why?" The disbelief in Grandfather's voice mirrored his own sentiments.

"It has always been about making *you* suffer. I wanted you to suffer for every unkind word. I wanted you to suffer for making me believe I wasn't good enough. I wanted you to suffer the way Mother did when you neglected her, when you cast her aside. She was always so unhappy."

"You don't know of what you speak." Grandfather's tone softened as he took another step closer to Daniel. He shook his head. "After you boys were born she was so happy. She wanted more children, talked of nothing else. But after several miscarriages, she became despondent, plunging into the depths of despair. No matter what I tried to do or say, she pushed me away." Sadness laced each word. "My heart broke the day she died."

Grandfather had suffered so much during the course of his life. It was no wonder he clung to whatever happiness was within his reach. Sabina may have convinced herself through the years that the events of the past had been her fault, but Maximus truly believed she saved his grandfather and mother from a lonely existence.

Uncle Daniel was visibly shocked by the revelation. Misery flashed in his eyes before it disappeared, turning into hatred. "You're lying!" He pointed a pistol at Grandfather. "I watched her suffer, heard her cry, felt her pain."

"I loved your mother." Grandfather's voice quivered.

Daniel ran one hand through his hair, grasping at its ends, while the other kept the pistol pointed firmly at Grandfather. "And what about me?"

"You're my son, of course I love you."

"Then why didn't you show it?" He waved the gun at Grandfather. "You always favored Martin, were always more interested in what he did or said."

Maximus didn't know what to do. One wrong move and Grandfather might die. There was no telling what Uncle Daniel was capable of.

"You put everyone before me." Uncle Daniel turned and pointed the pistol at Sabina. "Even her."

"No!" Maximus yelled as he started toward Sabina.

"I'd stay where you are or else watch your love die." Before Maximus could register what was happening, Uncle Daniel quickly maneuvered behind Sabina and pressed the pistol to her back.

A sharp gasp escaped her lips. Her eyes pleaded with Maximus.

"Daniel, put the gun down," Grandfather ordered in a firm, yet gentle tone. "Don't do this. We can talk—"

"I don't have to listen to you," defiance laced every word. "I don't..."

"No!" Mother's voice echoed from behind as Larentia called indiscernible words.

Everything happened all at once. Loud shouts, movement behind the trees, gunfire ringing through the air, followed by painful screams.

The world around Maximus faded. Panic like he'd never known hardened in his throat. Harsh pounding reverberated in his chest as he watched Sabina fall to the ground. Anger and concern intensified as he rushed toward her, sliding on the mud as he came to Sabina's side.

"Sabina?" Icy fear twisted around his heart as he reached for her.

"I'm fine," she whispered as her eyes fluttered open.

He took her in his arms and cradled her. "Where were you struck?"

"I wasn't." She reached up and stroked his cheek. "I heard someone yell to get down. I didn't know if that was meant for me, but I did."

Maximus looked around as if noticing his surroundings for the first time. Grandfather and Picus were huddled over Uncle Daniel's body, while Larentia stood to one side with a pistol in her hand.

"You shot him?" Maximus began to stand, bringing Sabina with him.

Larentia gazed down at the body, then met Maximus's eyes. "I had to stop him. I could not lose—"

"You're safe," Mother's cry reached his ears moments before he saw her push past the low brush. She rushed straight into his arms. "You're not injured?" She cupped his face and looked into his eyes. A long sigh rushed from her lips as tears streamed down her face. "You're safe."

"Larentia saved—"

For the second time in less than a few minutes, his mother interrupted. She went to Larentia and wrapped her arms around her. "You saved our son."

Our son. It warmed him to know that the woman who gave birth to him had accepted the woman who had raised him. He was blessed to have *two* wonderful mothers.

Grandfather stood and turned toward them. "He's dead." The words were heavy with sorrow and laced with regret.

Silence enveloped them.

Maximus released Sabina and went to his grandfather. Unsure what to say, he spoke from his heart. "Uncle Daniel would not have been satisfied until he carried out his revenge. I wish it hadn't ended like this—"

"I know." Grandfather inhaled deeply. On a long slow exhale, he said, "Ever since his mother died, he hasn't been the same. I had not a clue that he was so angry though. I..." Tears filled his eyes. "I wish..."

Maximus brought him within his embrace. "I know...I know." He patted his grandfather's back.

Grandfather stepped out of Maximus's arms. "Thank you, my boy," he whispered. He then sniffled back the tears, and masked his emotions before facing the others. "Once again, it would seem Miss St. Albans has saved our family." Larentia beamed with pride and protectiveness. "Thank you, Miss St. Albans, for protecting us."

Picus went to Larentia's side. "Do I dare ask how you learned to fire a pistol with such proficiency?"

"Let's just say Larentia was quite competitive when Grandfather St. Albans was instructing Lucius and me. She will not be bested by anyone with a pistol." Maximus ended with a wink.

"I knew one day you boys would get into some sort of trouble." She shook her head. "I always assumed Lucius would be at the source."

Laughter rang through the small clearing. Maximus hoped this was the start of a brighter future.

Chapter Fifteen

SABINA LAY WRAPPED within the folds of Maximus's arms, her body melting into his, content, and sated. Stroking her hand across his chest, she relished the feel of his firm muscles. The cottage had become their own little hideaway to escape the demands of everyday and indulge in their passion.

"I'm glad Larentia found love." Sabina wanted everyone to find and experience love the way she had with Maximus, albeit without all the tragedy. But sometimes tragedy brings with it the most precious of gifts.

"I would have never believed it in a thousand years..."

"Why?"

"She always said she was content with her life." Maximus paused. "Perhaps she was until she met Picus."

"Picus is a good man. He will take good care of her."

"I intend on taking good care of you," Maximus said in a seductive tone that promised to be her undoing.

She swirled her finger across his chest, then slowly traced the length of his birthmark.

"You have a tiny little mole at the bottom, right here," she said as she kissed the spot.

"I do? Huh, I never noticed it before."

"I wonder if your brother has the same mark." They had the same birthmark after all.

Maximus flipped Sabina on to her back. "That information will have to remain a mystery to you, *amore mia.*"

"Are you jealous?" she said with a tease.

"Not at all."

Sabina caressed his cheek. "You have nothing to be jealous of... ever. I fell in love with you." She kissed his cheek. "You saw past my flaws." She brushed a kiss to his lips and then flicked her tongue.

"*Ti amo.*"

"I love you, too." The words came so easy now. Everything in her life seemed so complete, even the nightmares had stopped thanks to Maximus. He'd been patient, kind, and loving as he listened to each and every one she'd ever had—her mind had never let her forget the turmoil of her youth. He brought her in closer to his warm body. She could have spent the rest of her life laying here just like this with Maximus, but he had obligations to fulfill. "Lord March, I do believe your guests await."

"They will be your guests as well, the soon-to-be Lady March." With everything that had happened, Sabina still could not believe they would be officially announcing their engagement this evening. Every day her love for him deepened and intensified.

His warm lips pressed softly against hers then gently covered her mouth, arousing every inch of her body. His arms encircled her, keeping their bodies close.

"Maximus," she murmured against his lips. As much as she wanted to continue, she didn't want to explain to Warrington or Sylvia what they'd been doing all afternoon. Sighing against his lips, she muttered, "We're going to be late." She could not wait till they were married and did not have to sneak around like this.

A frustrated sigh escaped his lips as he released her. Edging out of bed, she glanced over her shoulder. His seductive gaze followed her every movement, heating her body.

"*Maximus*, if you keep looking at me like that, we will be late. And *you* will have to explain to your mother."

"Alright," he exhaled with a huff as he got out of bed. "But as soon as we're married, I will not let you leave the bed so quickly."

"Promise?" She watched as he got dressed before she tended to her own clothing. His movements were manly, yet elegant. She would never tire of watching him.

Maximus's eyes caught hers as he turned around. "I think I better ready our horses or I may toss you back in bed and keep you there all night." He didn't wait for her to answer but strolled from the bedroom.

"I'll join you shortly."

Sabina finished dressing, and then tidied her hair the best she could, hoping no one would take notice of her disheveled appearance when she returned to the house. She was looking forward to a long hot bath before the soirée this evening.

Images of a relaxing bath were ruined by loud shouts drifting into the tiny cottage. "Damn you! You had no right ruining my sister."

Titus.

"I love her and plan to marry her." Even as Maximus's words touched her heart, panic rose from within. Her brother would not take this news well.

A moment later her fear was proven correct. "Over my dead body. You and your family can go to hell!"

Oh no!

Sabina ran outside, straight toward her brother and Maximus, positioning herself between them, arms outstretched.

"Go back inside, Sabina," her brother ordered in a commanding voice she didn't know he was capable of, he certainly never exerted such authority over his wife.

"No." She continued to hold her arms wide, keeping the men she loved at a short distance. "I love him."

"You can't possibly. Father is dead because of his family." Titus's breathing was heavy. "They've brought nothing but heartache to us."

"It's not their fault. His Grace lost his son, too. The entire situation was out of our control." Sabina tried to reason with Titus. "Father was a good man who was trying to help his friend. He would not want you suffering like this, Titus. Don't let anger consume you."

Silence enveloped them as her brother thought about Sabina's words. Anger had consumed Titus just as fear had consumed her all these years.

"Please don't make me choose between the men I love."

Titus lowered his fists, his features slightly relaxing. He continued to eye them both as he seemed to struggle for words. She knew his struggle. Sabina had many memories of their father, but Titus had been so little, he didn't remember how much Father had loved them. For the longest time, he only knew the lies their mother had weaved. It took years for Sabina to undo the destruction Mother had caused, but in the end, it had brought brother and sister closer together.

Maximus started to take a step forward, but Sabina shook her head.

Countless seconds more had passed before Titus finally spoke. "I don't want you to suffer any more than you already have, not if I can change it." He closed the distance and brought Sabina into a brotherly embrace. "I may not be thrilled with this union, but I don't want to be the cause of your unhappiness. You have my blessing."

"Thank you, Titus."

Epilogue

Five months later

"DEARLY BELOVED, WE *are gathered together here in the sight of God, to join together this man and this woman in holy matrimony...*"

The Vicar continued reading from The Book of Common Prayer as Maximus leaned in and whispered, "Have I told you how beautiful you look today?" There was something different about her, something he couldn't quite define, but made her even more unique, more beautiful...more.

A soft pink blush kissed Sabina's creamy cheek. "Shh, pay attention."

"*Therefore, if any man can show any just cause why they may not lawfully be joined together, let him now speak, or else hereafter forever hold his peace.*" A pleasant hush washed over the guests before the Vicar continued with the service.

Maximus took Sabina's hand and squeezed it gently. Although Sabina kept her gaze centered on the altar, her widening smile and darkening blush said it all. It seemed as if only yesterday they had exchanged their own wedding vows.

"*Forasmuch as Hereford William Picus and Larentia Rhea St. Albans have consented together in holy wedlock, and have witnessed the same before God and this company...*"

This company. The family chapel was filled with family and friends, here to celebrate this joyous union. Larentia had often said through the years that she never felt the need to marry, that she'd raised two adopted sons and that she wasn't missing anything in her life. But when Picus approached him and Lucius, asking for Larentia's hand, Maximus knew Larentia had found what she was missing.

Maximus watched the couple exchange loving glances. He knew Grandfather St. Albans was smiling down on them today, perhaps even chuckling at the sight of his only child—the same one who declared she would be a spinster forever—marrying. He had no doubt that Picus would make Larentia very happy.

With the ceremony complete, it was time for Maximus to sign his name as a witness to the register. Sabina excused herself, wanting to enjoy the fine early autumn day.

After the register was signed, Maximus rejoined Sabina, who was resting on a bench surrounded by rose bushes. Her features were flushed. He rushed to her side. "Are you ill?"

"I'm better, now," she said as she patted the spot beside her. "Sit with me while we wait for the others."

Better now? Fear laced his throat. Maximus slid next to his wife and brought her petite hand within his. "What's wrong?"

She looked at him curiously before she broke into laughter. "Oh dear. I didn't mean to alarm you." She cupped his cheek. "Nothing is wrong." She brushed a soft kiss across his cheek before whispering in his ear, "I'm with child."

Maximus pulled away and looked into the dual-colored eyes that still fascinated him so much. "Already? Are you sure? When? How?"

Laughter drifted from her lips. "I believe you have quite the understanding of how." She lowered her voice, "Especially after this morning." A little sigh escaped her lips. "Are you happy?"

Every so often Sabina still seemed unsure, as if their happiness was temporary. He couldn't blame her after everything she'd been through. He hoped with time, and the new life they were building together, all those fears could finally be laid to rest.

His lips brushed against hers as he spoke, "With you, always, *amore mia.*"

"*Ahem.*"

Maximus broke the kiss to find his brother standing in the near distance.

"Am I interrupting?" Lucius said as he limped toward them.

Although it had been five months Lucius still had not made a full recovery. But despite the slight limp and remnants of the gash across his face, he was still quite the rake, even here in the country. Ladies couldn't help but feel sorry for Lucius, and, in turn, his brother relished in the attention.

"My darling wife just informed me she is with child." Pride burst from his chest.

"Excellent. Excellent news indeed. And it works out quite well for me," Lucius said with a tease.

Sabina raised a delicate brow.

Lucius began to clarify, "Perhaps now Mother and Larentia will stop fussing so much."

"You are incorrigible, Lucius," Sabina said.

Lucius approached and took the empty seat beside Sabina. "With all sincerity, I am happy for you both. This truly *is* excellent news."

"What is excellent news?" Grandfather said as he exited the chapel.

"Have I missed something?" Mother quickly added as she strolled up to them.

However, before Maximus could say anything Larentia and Picus strolled from the chapel looking so happy, so in love.

Larentia glanced between the boys before questioning. "What are the two of you up to?"

Lucius stood and said with a half-smile, "For once, I am innocent of any and all accusations. It was all Maximus's doing...well, Maximus and Sabina's."

Everyone turned their full attention on them. Maximus looked at Sabina, who was smiling brightly. She nodded. Maximus took her hand as they stood together.

"Sabina is with child."

No sooner had the words left his mouth, they were swarmed with hugs. Laughter and well-wishes floated through the air as tears filled their eyes.

"I never thought I would live to see the day when, not only would I have my grandsons back in my life, but I would be a great-grandfather." Tears streamed down Grandfather's cheeks.

It had been an interesting journey, and one that Maximus suspected was just beginning. He was looking forward to this new adventure, surrounded by the people who loved them most in the world. Most of all, he was looking forward to starting his own traditions with the love of his life by his side. His one, his only love, his Sabina.

Chapter One Excerpt from:

Lady Soldier

A Legend To Love Series
Jillian Chantal

Chapter One

GALLOPING AT FULL speed with the wind blowing her hair out of its formerly neat and tidy style and sure she'd lost several ribbons in the process, The Honorable Matilda—Maud—Somerset almost flew over the neck of her horse when she pulled on the reins too hard.

Her mother standing on the porch of their country house, clearly agitated, was enough to cause Maud consternation. "It appears we're in trouble again, Khan."

Two grooms appeared. One took control of her large black horse and one assisted her off the animal's back.

As soon as she was on her feet, her mother strode over to her. In a tone as frosty as if were mid-January instead of July, said, "Would it be unreasonable for me to expect a bit of decorum from you? Here you are dressed again in some long-deceased female's gown you found in the attic and acting like a hoyden."

"I was merely exercising Khan. What harm is there in that?"

"When you've been told the mother and father of the young man your uncle and father have chosen as your potential groom are coming to call, I *do* expect you to be ready and properly attired." Her mother flicked one of the loose ribbons. "I blame your father. He should never have allowed you to learn about firearms, swords and crossbows. He's ruined you."

Glad she'd left the crossbow she'd been practicing with behind the folly, Maud pasted an apologetic smile on her face. "I'll go right up and change. I'm sorry, I forgot." She turned toward the front door.

Her mother grabbed her arm—a bit too tightly—and squeezed. "You'll use the servants' entrance. Our guests are already inside and you cannot walk past the morning room in that sorry state."

Maud knew her mother was right and even though she had no desire to marry, she knew she had to obey her parents. She plodded along, reluctant for the meeting to come.

Behind her, she heard her mother add, in a soft voice as she followed her own rule of a lady never raising hers, "And don't drag your feet in that manner. It's not attractive for a young lady to be heard arriving by the shuffling of her slippers."

Maud muttered under her breath, "Even in riding boots, I presume."

"I'm sorry, did you address me?" Her mother's tone was slightly brusquer than it had been.

Deciding there was nothing to gain by further discussion with her mother, Maud made haste to the servants' entrance.

As she walked through the back hallway, she passed a couple of maids who averted their eyes when they noticed her. They were used to her being in their domain by now. It seemed more and more that Maud was banished to the non-family side of the house. When she was under marriageable age, her father allowed her to learn the art of swordsmanship and other battle skills along with her brother. It hadn't been a problem to anyone in the house except her mother and older sister, but they tolerated it.

Until her sister became betrothed. Suddenly, it was urgent that Maud make a better impression in the county. After all, she was next to be on the auction block on the marriage mart. Hiding her natural love of the outdoors and its pursuits was well nigh impossible for her, but she was doing the best she could to suppress her natural tendencies.

In her quarters, the maid she and her sister still shared—at least until Charlotte's marriage—was pacing the area in front of the cold fireplace. "Miss Matilda, we must dress your hair and replace your gown. Miss Charlotte has already been here twice seeking you."

"I know, Mary. Mama stopped me outside and sent me up the back staircase." Maud let out a deep sigh and plopped into the chair in front of her dressing table. "Take out these cursed ribbons first and then we can choose my gown."

"Your mother has already chosen the dark blue one with the silver overskirt."

"That one again? One would think it's the only garment she thinks I own. She's always pressing me to wear it."

"It does show off your complexion and eyes to an advantage, Miss."

"You know how lucky you are not to have such a mother as I?" Maud glanced at Mary behind her in the looking glass. She noticed a shadow pass over the girl's face and immediately regretted her hasty words. She reached over her shoulder and took her maid's hand where it was busy taking the remnants of ribbon from her hair. "I'm sorry. I know your mother is no longer alive and that wasn't a kind thing I said."

"It's all right, Miss Matilda. I know you mean no harm. I can even understand your anger at your mother. As a servant, I don't have to worry about an arranged marriage. If it's not too forward of me to say so, I'm sorry this is happening to you."

Maud shrugged. "It's not like I'm the only one it happens to. When your uncle is a duke, no matter how far down the line you are, everyone has an idea on how your marriage can help the family. What the bride wants matters not at all."

"Miss Charlotte seems content with the choice made for her." As soon as the words passed Mary's lips, she clapped her hand to her mouth. "I shouldn't be impertinent."

Waving her hand in the air, Maud said, "It makes no difference to me." She smiled at her maid. "Charlotte has always been Mama's favorite. She accepts everything decided for her and learned to do her needlework and play the piano beautifully. I'm the disappointment."

"Oh no, miss. All of us in the household are quite fond of you and your bravery."

Her hair was finally free of the old ribbons and Maud stood and held her arms out, knowing she'd need to be washed off before stepping into her fresh gown. "Unfortunately, that quality is not one that is desirable in a female."

Mary nodded and moved over to the ewer and basin. "We should hurry. Someone will be sent to fetch you momentarily."

Maud knew she was right and stood in silence as she was made ready to return downstairs to be assessed by her prospective groom's family like a fatted calf. It was all she could do not to cry. She hadn't even been told who was being considered. How was that reasonable? Knowing the women in her family had been subjected to these kind of marriages since at least before the ancestress she was named for, Queen Maud, didn't make her any happier about the fact it was happening to her in her own turn.

When she was properly attired, Maud ran down the corridor, hoping neither her mother nor sister would see her. They always moved at a proper, sedate pace and would surely lecture her on her deportment.

At the door to the front parlor, she stopped, took a deep breath and ran her right hand over her hair.

Myers, the butler, nodded a question at her and she smiled. "I think I'm prepared."

With that, he opened the door with a flourish.

Six sets of eyes turned to scrutinize her. Blood rushed to her ears and all sound stopped except the roaring in her veins.

Of course she knew her parents, uncle and sister. The other couple, she'd never seen before. They appeared amiable with their smiling faces, but she knew she was like one of the insects on display the last time she visited the British Museum. She was sure they were judging her harshly for keeping them waiting.

Her uncle, the Duke of Beaufort, stepped over to her with his hands extended. "Ah, Matilda. Come and meet Lord and Lady Davison. He's a baron."

So it was possible the marriageable son would have a title someday which Maud supposed was a good match for the niece of a current duke and granddaughter of the prior one. But why wasn't the potential groom present? Could he be as reluctant as she for such a contract?

She curtsied and, in a demure voice she knew her mother would approve, she said, "Very pleased to meet you both."

Lady Davison smiled slightly, but her husband still had a frown furrowing his brow.

Knowing her mother would never forgive her if she didn't at least *try* to charm these people who might very well one day be her family, Maud offered to do the one thing she was talented at in the drawing room. "If Mama would accompany me on the pianoforte, I'd love to sing some of my favorite songs for you."

"You mean you don't play?" Lord Davison's brow furrowed even more if that were possible. Now it looked like a big brown centipede was perched above his eyes. Maud choked back a laugh.

"Yes. She plays, but she loves the singing so much, she sometimes accidentally skips a note or two in her enthusiasm for the words." Coming to her daughter's rescue, her mother led her to the pianoforte.

She whispered in Maud's ear, "You sing like you've never sung before. Don't disappoint your uncle."

Not for the first time in her life did Maud wish she was a duke. It must be a wonderful way to live. Everyone wanting to make sure you, and only you, were happy.

"Would you prefer to hear *Meet Me by Moonlight* or *The Last Rose of Summer*?" Maud asked her audience who had all taken seats in the gilded gold and white upholstered chairs.

"How about both?" the duke asked.

Knowing she needed to impress the Davisons with her voice, since judging by the sour look on the baron's face, he didn't appear to be going to forgive her for her lack of piano skills, Maud took a deep breath and nodded at her mother to begin the first song.

As she sang, she watched their faces. Lady Davison seemed pleased with the ballad, but her husband still had a frown. Maud idly wondered if his beetled brow was his regular expression. Perhaps the man didn't like anything he could see of the world.

When the song was over, everyone politely clapped.

"One more, Matilda and then we'll go into the dining room for some refreshments," the duke said. He inclined his head to her and she did as he bade and moved into the next song, one recently adapted from an old Irish melody. She smiled to herself as she sang. This song was special to her as the old melody had been a favorite of her brother's.

Before she finished the second stanza to start the third, a blond head popped in the open window and, in an instant, Maud knew she'd never marry Mr. Davison. Not that she'd wanted to marry a stranger, but now she was sure things were going to go seriously awry.

No one but she had noticed the man since the others had their backs to the wall of windows looking out on the lawn. She tried to subtly shake her head to discourage him from speaking.

Luck was not on her side, as Sanderson Grimes, never known for his discretion, called out, "What did I tell you about singing that Irish tune, trusty trout?"

Shocked as Maud's parents, sister, uncle and two strangers turned as one to gape at him, Sanderson regretted his interruption. He hadn't realized the family had visitors. Blundering in was one of the things he tended to do, but he'd been so excited to be on leave from the army, he'd dashed over from his family's estate almost as soon as he left his kit bag. He'd missed his friend and wanted to see her.

Not paying close attention, he'd merely thought she was singing for her own enjoyment and had somehow mastered the skill of piano playing in his absence.

And now here he was, obviously interrupting something very important if the rage on Maud's uncle's face was any indication.

Making the Duke of Beaufort angry was certainly not on his list of things to do this day when he'd been riding through the countryside, but it appeared he'd certainly done so.

Trying to make the best of the blunder he made, Sandy said, "I'm so sorry to have interrupted your musical interlude. I've just returned from my regiment and wanted to greet the family."

"And now you have, so please excuse us, Grimes," the duke said.

Casting a glance at his good friend, Maud, Sandy backed away from the window. The expression on her face caused him no little consternation. He'd never wish ill on her, but now he was sure she would be the one to pay the price for his error. He hoped the duke wasn't prone to violence on women. Not that he'd ever heard any rumors to that effect, but one never knew.

He walked off the porch and around the side of the manor to the stables. It was Maud's special place and Sandy knew she'd come as soon as she could.

Settling in for a long wait as he knew the duke wouldn't be in a hurry to cut short his visit, he leaned against a bale of hay near one of the stalls.

A stable hand came upon him there, but merely doffed his cap and moved on to mucking out one of the stalls farther down the row.

Sandy closed his eyes and found himself dozing off once or twice. Shaking his head to stay awake, after what seemed to be an hour, he finally decided she wasn't going to be able to manage to slip away.

He stood and wiped some stray straw from the seat of his breeches just as she came around the corner. She smacked into his chest, causing him to step backward as he caught her by the elbows. "Slow down."

"Thank goodness you haven't gone yet." Maud took his arm. "Come with me. My uncle is readying to leave and I don't want him to see you again."

"He was not best pleased to see me, was he?"

"Not in the least." She dragged him to the far end of the stable block. "Those people were here to inspect me and even before your inauspicious entrance, I wasn't making a great impression."

"Inspecting you?"

"It seems I'm next to be betrothed in my family."

"I didn't see a potential groom in there. Or did I miss him? Was he hiding in the corner behind your mother's fake shrubbery?" Sandy smiled, but he wasn't happy this was happening to his friend. She deserved so much more than it seemed she was getting. He knew she hated being her uncle's pawn as if she were a chess piece.

"It appears he cannot be bothered to make a search for his own bride." She shook her head as tears filled her eyes. "I imagine if his parents approved of me, he's in the same position as I am. No chance to say no."

"But you think they didn't approve even before I came in and ruined it all?"

"While the duke is angry at you and perhaps will blame you if they say they aren't interested in me as a daughter-in-law, I'm sure the putative groom's father didn't care for me at all. The sneer he greeted me with never left his face."

"I can't tell how you feel about this turn of events, Maud. Are you happy you probably won't be marrying a stranger or are you sad that you won't?"

"As you know, I have no desire to marry. What I'm sad about is my family being angry at me."

He pulled her to him and gave her a hug. They'd been friends for so many years, she was like a sister to him and he hated she was hurting. "Did they yell too badly after I disappeared?"

"No. It was worse than that. The room became eerily quiet and still. I tried to return to the song, but Mama stopped playing. As soon as she did, the duke and my father led the Davisons out of the parlor."

"What happened then?"

"Once they were out of the room, Mama started crying. It broke my heart, Sandy. I've certainly caused my mother some grief in our lives—especially with my love of firearms and crossbows—but I think this was the first time I realized just how much she despairs of me."

"I know you hate to hurt your mother. We all do, but we all must also remain true to ourselves."

Maud shook her head. "No, my friend, *we* don't. Men are allowed to be true to themselves. Women are not. You and I both know it."

Sandy knew she was right. It was the way of the world. It would do no good for him to try to convince her otherwise.

End of Excerpt Lady Soldier (A Legend to Love series) by Jillian Chantal

A Legend To Love Series

Between Duty and the Devil's Desires
by Louisa Cornell

When the Marquess Returns by Alanna Lucas

Lady Soldier by Jillian Chantal

My Wild Irish Rogue by Saralee Etter

The Lady and Lord Lakewood by Aileen Fish

His Duchess at Eventide by Wendy La Capra

A Wulf in Duke's Clothing by Renée Reynolds

The Promise of the Bells by Elizabeth Ellen Carter

Rogue of the Greenwood by Susan Gee Heino

A Gift From A Goddess by Maggi Andersen

The Duke of Darkness by Cora Lee

About the Author

Multi-published historical romance author Alanna Lucas grew up in Southern California, but always dreamed of distant lands and bygone eras. From an early age, she took an interest in history and travel, and is thrilled to incorporate those diversions into her writing. Alanna writes Regency-set historical romance.

When she is not daydreaming of her next travel destination Alanna can be found researching, spending time with family, or going for long walks. She makes her home in California with her husband, children, one sweet dog, and hundreds of books.

Just for the record, you can never have too many shoes, handbags, or books. And travel is a must.

If you'd like to find out more about Alanna or her books you can visit her website: www.alannalucas.com

Other Books by Alanna Lucas

Face to Face (In His Arms, Book One)
A masquerade, a chance meeting, and a kidnapping:
Little did Miss Penelope Ashurst realize that breaking
the rules would result in the adventure—and love—of a
lifetime.

When We Dance (In His Arms, Book Two)
Nigel Rochefort succeeds at everything he attempts,
but burying his family in scandal and breaking up a
wedding while seducing the bride is not *quite* what he
had in mind. Nor was finding true love.

Only a Hero Will Do
A beautiful, feisty heiress. A dashing, enigmatic, ex-
army captain. They must work together to defeat dark
forces threatening Britain's monarchy. Elizabeth Atwell
can break any code—but will she also break Grant
Alexander's heart?